SARAH SPADE

MURDER IN MOONBURROW
BOOK ONE

FOREWORD

Thank you for checking out *Fake It 'Til You Mate It*!

This book has been such a labor of love for me. I've always wanted to write my version of a cozy mystery (so expect some profanity and a little on-page spice!), and while I love cats, I thought: why not have the sidekick character be an *opossum*? Even better, why not make the *heroine* an opossum? Once I established that prey shifters—like opossums, porcupines, and skunks—were in my shifter universe when Bridget was sent to Dyea, Alaska in *Watch Me Burn,* I ran with the character opossum of Jenny—and Honey is the result! A happy-go-lucky yet anxious as anything heroine who has the tendency to 'play dead' at the worst moments, and is searching for a new start in the cozy small shifter town of Moonburrow.

Of course, since this is a murder mystery, things

aren't as sweet as they seem—though Honey's future mate might disagree with that... especially once he knows that Honey belongs to him. And when Max *does*? This Alpha will do anything to keep her—and keep her alive, too.

Fake It 'Til You Mate It relies on the fated mate trope, instalove, over-the-top scenarios, non-graphic murder, and a HEA despite the, well, murder(s).

I hope you enjoy it, and welcome to Moonburrow!

xoxo,
Sarah

PROLOGUE

If I had a nickel for every time I played possum and ended up in the morgue, I'd be fifteen cents richer, which might not seem like much, but really? After the second time I scared the shit out of the morgue technician, you'd think they might recognize me before popping me in the morgue drawer.

The way I'm surrounded by steel, refrigerated air pumping in from who-knows-where, my nose numb and my ass just about frozen solid tells me: yeah, not so much.

I'm on my back, arms trapped at my sides. It's dark, though one of the perks of being any sort of shifter is amazing night vision. I know exactly where I am, and even if this isn't the third time this has happened to me since I've lived in Glenville, the sterile air with notes of industrial cleaner make it obvious.

At least there *is* some air. Most of these drawers are airtight due to the stare of some of the real dead bodies —even humans can't mistake the truly nasty stink that comes with decomp—and if I'd stayed 'dead' much longer, that state could become way more permanent than I'd like. There's still some oxygen, so that's a plus, especially since I don't plan on staying in here until that happens.

It's fucking *cold* in the morgue drawer. If it wasn't for my inner beast—and my built-in fur coat—I might've lost a finger or two already. Last time, I woke up in the body bag before they moved me. The previous morgue tech nearly had a coronary when I cleared my throat and asked them to unzip me. He was new, too. After the first whoopsie, the long-time medical examiner shrugged off her lab coat and decided to retire to Hawaii. If my second resurrection affected her successor the same way, I'm probably going to have to figure out how to explain this to the latest hire.

Right. Because in a world where supernaturals—or supes—are a closely guarded secret unless you live in a

Fang City or belong to either a sanctuary or a pack town, I can just tell the poor, unsuspecting mortals that I'm an opossum shifter with a hint of witch on my mother's side, and I have a tendency to 'play dead' when startled.

It's only *playing*, though. You'd think an ME would know the difference between a woman in a catatonic-state and one who was, you know, *dead* dead.

The freezing cold morgue drawer tells me: nah.

I wiggle my big toe, squinting down the length of my prone body.

Yup. My shoes are gone, and there's a tag on it.

Don't slam your head against the steel drawer, Honey, I tell myself, since I don't want to knock out again. It was bad enough that I heard a car backfire when I was crossing over Main and Third, heading to get a croissant sandwich from the deli a block from the grocery store where I work as a cashier. I've managed to keep my supe status under wraps since I moved to the human town after graduating high school more than a decade ago. Rare as we are compared to the predators, prey shifters have always been at the bottom of the food chain. At least, living among humans, I didn't have to deal with shifter politics.

That's the plus. The downside? Is that, when a car backfires and my opossum instincts take over, I drop and, *whoops*, now I'm in the morgue.

Again.

Thankfully, I'm still dressed. The first time I dropped in front of a crowd of humans, the EMTs pronounced me dead on scene before shipping me off to the local morgue. The medical examiner didn't even wait until my family was informed of my 'heart attack' before she stripped me down, putting me on ice until she could autopsy me.

That was fun. I'd kicked my way out of the drawer, wrapping the sheet they covered me with around my body, asking meekly for my clothes while Dr. Hamm gaped at me, struggling to accept what she was seeing. No shoes this go-round, but I'm not naked, so that's one thing in my favor. If luck's really on my side, it's lunchtime for the medical examiner's office and I can sneak out before anyone sees me.

Claws crossed.

Scooting down a little, I brace my arms against the cold steel and rear my knees up as high as I can, then kick. Opossums don't have the impressive shifter strength like bears or wolves do, but I'm still powerful enough to snap the drawer open on my second try.

The drawer crashes open, the force of my kick sending it yanking outward with a squeaky squeal.

I pop my upper half up, grabbing the sides of the drawer, ready to push the rest of me out.

A startled gasp has my head swiveling to my right.

Crud.

I don't know if she's the new medical examiner or a

morgue attendant. Based on her youthful face, low ponytail, and the look of horror she's currently wearing, I'm thinking attendant. She had a tray of tools in her hand that clank against the tile as she drops them before lifting her hand, pointing a shaky finger at me.

I wave.

Her eyes widen.

"You're…"

A natural blonde with equally natural violet eyes that tip off my supernatural side?

"You're…"

An opossum shifter who is beginning to think she should just go furry and flee?

"You're…"

Not dead?

"*Alive.*"

Yup. Should've known it was that last one.

I shrug impishly. "Sorry."

I have too much color in my cheeks to be a zombie, I guess. Either that or the poor attendant never expected the undead to apologize. Her eyes roll back in her head, her body collapsing in on itself before she ends up in a puddle on the floor, as unconscious as I was after the car backfired right behind me.

That's my cue.

Forget the shoes. I have no idea where my phone is, and I'm only hoping that my driver's license and debit card are still in my back pocket instead of in a bag set aside for my next of kin—

Ah, hell. *Mom.* The first time, I got lucky. Dad answered the phone and, a full-blooded opossum shifter himself, he knew not to be worried when he got the call that I had 'died'. Mom's half opossum, half witch. She understands how sometimes our inner animal takes over, but she'd lectured me the second time on how dangerous it was to get caught out. Humans... it's better if they don't know that supernaturals exist all around them.

Plenty of prey shifters can live a normal life among their human neighbors. Raccoons, rabbits, rats... no problem. But us opossums? If she finds out that I got picked up *again*, I'll never hear the end of it.

She wants me to return home. To Virginia, where most of our clan has a tendency to stick around. She wants me to find a nice male to settle down with, whether he's my fated mate or not, and start popping out some opossum babies. And, no, Gus doesn't count according to my mother...

Pass.

So maybe I don't really know what I want to do with my life. I've been drifting along, taking whatever jobs I can find, determined not to return home until I've become someone to be proud of. Most prey shifters choose their mates instead of waiting for 'the one', but while I'm open to finding love, I'm not exactly looking.

Not yet. I'm happy living in my studio apartment with the perfect roommate, and... I don't know. It's possible the lack of oxygen in the drawer did get to me, but I'm beginning to think Mom has a point.

A tiny one.

Like, maybe it's time I give up trying to live as a human. I'm not a human. Not really. I'm a supe. I'm an opossum shifter.

And if I don't get out of here real soon, I have a lot of explaining to do.

I stop to make sure that the poor attendant is as comfortable as I can make her, and that she didn't faint on top of any of those sharp instruments she was carrying. Then, bending down, I slip the toe tag off, reading it. **H. Morgan** with the accurate date of birth. Great. They know who I am.

Peachy.

I slip the tag in my back pocket, muttering a soft curse when I pat them both, realizing they're empty. Just like I thought. Everything I was walking around with when I dropped must be in a bag somewhere.

I don't shift. It's bad enough that they'll have to explain a missing body. If I go furry and leave pieces of clothing all over the morgue, that will lead to even more questions.

They have my ID. The human police will show up at my apartment, and while I explained away my first two trips to the morgue as a result of a severe narcoleptic disorder, I don't think they'll buy it for a third time.

Honestly? I'm still not sure how I got away with it the *first* time.

Ah, well. Time to go, Honey. I spare a quick search around the pristine surroundings for my belongings, then decide it doesn't matter. Clock's ticking. I should probably hightail out of the morgue.

As I tiptoe toward the door, peeking through the small window, slipping out in my bare feet once I'm sure it's clear, I can't help but think I should probably think about leaving Glenville behind, too.

CHAPTER 1
MOONBURROW

Cupcakes saved my life—or, at the very least, gave me a jumpstart on new one.

Grabbing the jar of sprinkles, pinching a few between my fingers and letting them settle on the pink frosting, I think about how ridiculous that sounds. It's true. Discovering that I have a knack for baking—bread, pies, pastries, but cupcakes in particular—was the second biggest shock I received after I relocated from Glenville to Moonburrow.

Should I have been surprised? Probably not. Grandma Jean is a full-blooded witch, but that's just what kind of supe she is. My whole life, she's been a baker, and while I hadn't seen her in person since I left home the first time, that's how I remember her: the scent of sugar and magic following in her wake as me and Ash scampered behind that, begging her for a treat.

My cousin was related to me on my dad's side, but Grandma Jean didn't care. She fed her little 'possums, and my biggest regret after I moved to Glenville was that I only got goodies sent to me through the mail instead of fresh out of her oven.

Did I have any idea that I could make treats of my own? Considering I was a whizz at nuking up some dinners or boiling a pot of water for pasta and that was basically it, not even a little. That all changed when the fallout from being toe-tagged, then rising from the dead... *again*... meant that the Glenville Police had more than a few questions for me.

I'm not the biggest fan of the police, human or supe. I never have been, and I was willing to do anything to stay off their radar.

Too bad that Mom got the initial call. She already sent over the forged documentation about my narcolepsy, but the cops came by for a nice chat anyway. By the time I finally had them off my back, I agreed with my parents: I needed to be around my own kind. They meant opossums. I just meant supes.

And that's why, instead of returning to Virginia, I needed a backup plan.

I needed my grandmother.

Supes are long-lived. Vamps are basically immortal, while witches can last up to three centuries before they slow down; shifters get about half that. I don't know how old Grandma Jean is exactly. I do know, however, that Grandpa Gary shifted to an opossum one last time before I was born, then fell asleep. He reached the end, and while you wouldn't look at Grandma Jean and think her a day over sixty, Mom told me she was getting ready to move on.

Me being, well, *me*, I freaked. I thought she was dying. Silly Honey. Grandma Jean simply decided to do a tour of Europe, visiting old friends from the coven where she spent her formative years in France before moving to the United States and falling for my grandfather. Mom thought that was good for her, but that left the question: what would happen to Grandma Jean's bakery?

She opened Dough You Believe in Magic a few years ago. It's not her first bakery. When I was growing up, she owned a fancy patisserie in Northern Virginia. After I left home, so did she, settling in a small supernatural town where her patrons were happy to eat some of her charmed pastries as long as she stayed away from black magic and curses.

I'm impulsive. Always have been, and I doubt that's

going to change now. I offered to take the bakery—and the cozy apartment built on top of it—off of Grandma Jean's hands. Sure, I'd have to move to Moonburrow, but with that being only a couple of hours away from Mom and Dad, they begrudgingly agreed it was a good idea.

Not that it mattered. Grandma Jean loved the idea, and if Grandma Jean approved, not even Mom would argue with the matriarch of our immediate clan.

That's how, two months ago, I was given the keys to the bakery and the apartment, Grandma Jean's leather-bound book of recipes, and her blessing to do my best to take over Dough You Believe in Magic.

And it's been *great*.

For the most part, I've loved living in Moonburrow, Maryland. A shifter-run town, there's enough of a coven presence to charm it against humans. It's not on any map. Drivers coming this way inevitably find that there's a detour to take around it. You can't even get past the borders unless you have supe blood, but since it's also the home to the Moonshadow Pack, that means vampires are out. The long-standing Claws and Fangs war—between the predatory wolf shifters and their natural enemy, the fanged corpses—might be in a lull right now, but so long as we rely on the Alpha-led pack to protect the rest of us, Moonburrow keeps humans *and* vampires out.

If only it kept out sticky-fingered raccoons...

The front door to the bakery is kept locked until I open up for business at exactly eight o'clock. It's only seven-thirty now, but there's no denying I've been joined by Roxy Kane, who must have slunk in through the back door. How else can I explain her sudden appearance? Unlike me, she doesn't have a drop of witch blood, but there she is, joining me behind the counter, her black hair—and its trademark white stripes—up in a messy bun, while wearing ripped leggings, a leather jacket over her latest graphic tee, all topped off with an intense pair of sunglasses she's wearing indoors just because she's *that* kind of raccoon.

Or maybe she's doing something to hide the dark circles under her eyes that are part of what she is, same as how my purple eyes give me away to anyone who knows anything about opossum shifters...

Before it hits me that she's really there, she's reaching around me, her arm halfway into my pastry case.

"Morning." She waves with the hand *not* full of a chocolate croissant as she straightens up. "I'm testing your wares again." A large bite from the croissant and a hint of a smirk on her face as she chews before she says, "Still good."

I swat at her with my nearest counter rag. "Roxy! You can't just walk in and take pastries!"

"I didn't *just* take them." She bites into it again with obvious defiance. "I'm taste-testing. Big difference."

Sensing mine, Gus chitters in annoyance from his flour-bag throne.

"Oh, look." Roxy smirks. "It's your emotional support rat."

Gus shows the raccoon shifter his fangs.

She bares her teeth back at my baking partner because, yup, maturity is as dead as Gus will seem to be if she frightens him into appearing lifeless. She might be considered a prey shifter as a raccoon, but add her size and her attitude, and I wouldn't blame Gus for thinking she's a predator.

I roll my eyes, sparing a quick reassuring pat to Gus's head. "He's an opossum, and you know that."

Of course she does. *I'm* an opossum, and back when we were in high school together, she never let me forget it. It didn't matter that Onancock—and, yes, that's the name of the small Virginia town I grew up in—was heavy with opossum clans. Roxy is... well, she's *Roxy.*

She shrugs. "Right. Sorry. It's just... the tail thing. He looks like an oversized rat."

"Roxy—"

"Besides," she says, brushing crumbs off her leather jacket, changing the subject, "I was just swinging by before you open to—"

"Steal baked goods?"

"Support local small businesses," is her quipped response. She laughs. "With the utmost enthusiasm."

I sigh, fighting a small smile. That's the closest I can get to getting the feisty raccoon to admit that she is a big fan of my baking. "Fine. I can comp you one pastry a week. Not one every time I catch you with your paw in my display case."

"Oh, Honey." Roxy pats my arm like I'm adorable. "It's cute that you think that you're catching me instead of me showing you that I can get anything I want when I want it."

I can't help myself. I laugh, shaking my head.

Running into Roxy Kane is the *third* shock I received when I moved to Moonburrow. Last I heard, she was still skulking around Virginia, so when I picked up her familiar scent a few days after I arrived, I couldn't believe I accidentally followed my childhood nemesis to the same shifter town.

But I did, and if I hadn't forgotten how much Roxy teased and poked me when we were young shifters, she might've. At the very least, she seemed almost glad to see me when we actually met, though that could've been because she had someone to be her rascally raccoon self around.

Like, oh, *now*.

Moving around to the front of the display, she leans against my counter as though she belongs there. "So how goes it? The bakery thing working out? Moonburrow not as bad as you thought when you first caught me poking around your dumpster?"

True. I caught Roxy's scent, convinced myself I was imagining it, but when her head popped out of my dumpster, I couldn't deny that it was her.

"Yeah." I fiddle with the ends of one of my twin braids. "Things are going great."

Roxy studies me for a moment, her yellow eyes gleaming as though she can see something that I've spent two months trying to hide.

Here's hoping she *can't*.

Seconds later, she shrugs as she rises from her lean. "Good."

"Really?"

"Yeah. Why not? It might be nice to have someone around town that I actually tolerate."

I pretend to swoon. "Oh, Roxy. That's the sweetest thing you've ever said to me."

She shrugs. "That's because I snagged a cupcake while you weren't looking."

Lifting her hand, she wags the cupcake that I'd just finished frosting and covering in sprinkles before she graced me with her presence.

"Anyway," she says, "if you need someone to steal recipes, intimidate rude customers, dispose of bodies…"

Ah, jeez. *Roxy…*

"I'm running a bakery, not committing any felonies."

She raises the cupcake a little higher, toasting me with it. "Both require good instincts and a pinch of luck. You've got this."

Honestly? I'm not really sure how I'm supposed to respond to that, especially not when the comment came from *Roxy Kane*, so I just shoot her a bewildered look. "Thanks." I pause. "I think."

Roxy removes the cupcake liner, flinging it over to where Gus is—as usual—perched on his bag of flour, whiskers twitching. He hisses as the liner just misses him before burying his snout in the paper, searching for a few crumbs to devour and the traces of frosting to lick.

Another shake of my head. "Don't tease Gus."

"Don't keep your pet rat in the bakery where you can get fur in the croissants," is her cheeky retort.

Ignoring the way she's teasing by calling Gus a rat again, the reality is that I *have* to. I don't really have a choice. Ever since Gus imprinted on my opossum, treating me like a member of his brood, I've been stuck with him. I was lucky I could convince him to wait at the apartment when I went to work at the grocery store. Now that I live over the bakery, there's no way I can keep him from joining me downstairs.

Not that I would if I could. Roxy might know that

I'm an opossum shifter, but I'd rather keep that to myself for the moment. That means, if my scent-dampener charm fails, I have the excuse of blaming Gus for the *eau de possum* aroma permeating the bakery beneath the scents of yeast, cinnamon, vanilla, and sugar.

Besides, that's one of the best things about a shifter-run town. When you can never tell if an animal is a resident in their fur or their wild counterpart, who's to say that I can't keep an opossum in my bakery? There's no health department in Moonburrow, and a little fur never hurt anyone—especially when the fur she's picking out of her teeth could be her own.

I keep all of that to myself, though. My former frenemy might have grown up over the last decade, becoming someone that *I* can tolerate, but it's better if I keep my own secrets.

So I just wave her off as she heads toward the front door, the still untouched cupcake in her hand, waiting for her to take a bite. "See ya."

"Make almond croissants tomorrow!"

I don't even dignify that with a response to the pastry thief. Instead, I grab another cupcake and my jar of sprinkles, replacing the one that Roxy snagged from the display.

She must have stopped at the door because it's still shut as she calls out, "Oh, and Honey?"

I look up.

"I should tell you that your back door lock sucks.

Anyone could have broken in, not just a talented raccoon."

With that last remark, Roxy disappears out the front door before I can come up with a retort to that.

Next to me, Gus pointedly uses his paw to knock that mangled, chewed cupcake liner to the floor. He chitters, and I can't help but interpret his regal complaint without, you know, actually speaking 'opossum' while I'm in my skin.

I boop his nose. "Don't mind Roxy, bud. She's always like that."

CHAPTER 2
CAN'T RESIST CUPCAKES

WHAT A WASTE OF PERFECTLY GOOD TREATS…

IT'S OKAY. I'LL GET THEM FROM THE TRASH LATER.

— GUS

Every few days, I try to make a new recipe from my grandmother's book to give away as free samples. It was a way to introduce myself to the town while assuring Grandma Jean's customers that I have just enough of her magic to run the shop while she's overseas.

After Roxy's unexpected visit this morning, I got a later start than usual. I didn't even start searching for one that sounded interesting until after I sold out of the chocolate croissants that Roxy 'taste-tested', but when I saw that Grandma Jean named the recipe Can't Resist Cupcakes, I knew that's the one I wanted to try.

I don't have as much magic as Grandma Jean, but most of her recipes don't call for it apart from some unique herbs and powders that you wouldn't normally find in pastries—but when I follow her recipes exactly, they come out pretty damn good, if I do say so myself.

The Can't Resist Cupcakes have a lemon filling and strawberry buttercream frosting. I garnish them with some candied lemon slices and set them out on the free sample tray in between customers. Because I got slammed directly after, I didn't even have a chance to try them myself before I was too busy. Next thing I know, I was bagging up a loaf of rye bread for Mrs. Carlson, a sweet hedgehog shifter who was friends with my grandmother while the rest of the rush either looked at my display case or mosied their way over to the free sample table.

I had at least five customers milling around it— including a wolf shifter who, as a predator, had my nerves twanging—when the first cupcake kicked in.

It was Sondra who ate it. A squirrel shifter with a high metabolism who works for the Moonburrow postal service, she brushes a chunk of soft grey hair out of her dark eyes and announces, "I hide acorns under my pillow in case I get hungry in the middle of the night. When Willie"—her rat shifter mate—"starts to snore, I drop them on top of his forehead until he stops."

Um. Okay. Not something I was expecting her to share, but I get it. I've never slept in bed with anyone other than Gus, but if he ever started to snore, I might nudge him in the side until he gave it up.

"I dye my fur," blurts out the red-haired shifter that I've seen come into the shop once or twice. Her pointed face and coloring tells me she's a fox. "I've always wanted to be a vibrant shade of orange and the drug store just outside of town sells it in a box."

Her hands fly up to her face, cheeks pinkening.

My stomach drops. What the...

Lara, a pretty witch with bouncy blonde curls, might've snickered to hear the fox shifter's unexpected confession, but that was before she finished taking a bite out of her own cupcake.

One bite. That's all it took. One bite and her soft green eyes go slightly glassy as she says conversationally, "I cursed the printer in my boss's office. Whenever he wants to waste paper on another ridiculous memo, it jams and then—" She blinks suddenly, looking down at the cupcake she just took a bite out of. "Hang on. What kind of cupcakes are these, Honey? One of your grandmother's recipes?"

Uh-oh.

Can't Resist Cupcakes. I just... I thought it meant that my customers 'can't resist' enjoying their flavor.

Um. No. That's not it.

Not at all.

They can't resist blurting out their secrets.

Truth bombs. Holy shit, Honey. You just served *truth bombs* to your customers.

I hope I'm wrong. I hope *she's* wrong. But when the amber-eyed wolf shifter I pointedly pretended not to notice prowling around the bakery starts saying something about the Alpha and my heart drops, it doesn't matter. I shut down when it comes to anything to do with that male. Max Lobo, that is, and not the fair-haired wolf who is popping the second half of the cupcake into his mouth.

No!

Mrs. Carlson reaches to grab one from the sample tray on her way out of the bakery.

I point, then hiss under my breath, "Gus. Get 'em!"

The wily opossum immediately leaps to the floor, his long tail trailing behind him as he heads for the sample tray. He's quick. In no time, he's spiraled up the stand, hooking his teensy claws on the edge of the table, and leaping onto the tray.

Gus buries his face in the nearest cupcake. That's okay. I'm not worried about him spilling his guts, even if I'm more concerned about him adding to his pudgy belly by feeding him all that sugar.

Ah, well. It can't be helped.

His snout is in one cupcake. His right paw is

covered in frosting from another. Even his tail dips past the frosting of a third, digging into the cake. When he pulls it out, it'll be covered in lemon filling, but at least the Can't Resist Cupcakes won't be messing with my neighbors any longer.

Thank you, Gus.

Mrs. Carlson draws her hand back. From one supe to another, she'll never judge me for keeping an opossum in here, but that doesn't mean she's still interested in a cupcake.

Phew.

Racing around the counter, I pull a stern expression to my face, wagging my finger at Gus. "Bad Gus. Those were for our friends."

Gus doesn't understand English. Not really. He's an opossum after all, and I've had three different witches verify that he's not a shifter in disguise. But while I can understand the gist of what he means, same goes for me—though, if I'm being fair, Gus is way better at understanding me than I am him.

Which is why he doesn't seem upset that I'm scolding him. Or maybe that's just Gus being Gus because he gives me a mischievous look before darting his tongue out, licking the frosting from his whiskers...

Either way, I use the distraction to grab the tray. Hurrying behind the counter, I drop the plate of cupcakes into the trash before any more of my customers can get caught in the spell and confess some of their deepest darkest secrets to me.

And then I grin.

"Who wants to try one of the eclairs I was just about to fill instead?"

I HOPED THAT THE SNAFU FROM THIS MORNING WENT unnoticed. That my customers were grateful for a fresh batch of eclairs on the house, and that they went on their merry ways, not realizing that they blabbed about more than they would've ever wanted to.

If only.

The bakery slows down in the early afternoon. There's always a small rush near close when customers come in for the last of the daily bread for their dinners, but in the three-hour gap between lunchtime and when I get ready to close for the evening, it's usually slow enough for me to start some of the bakes for tomorrow morning.

I tried to pretend like it was a good thing today, and not like rumors from the morning rush meant that Moonburrow locals were avoiding my shop. Optimistic... that's me. And if I'm nervous-baking some cinnamon sandies while I work to keep from peeking out into the street... well, at least I'll have something delicious to snack on after I slink back upstairs with Gus.

I'm just measuring out the flour when the other shoe drops.

A familiar scent of woodsy pine and something sharp slaps me in the face so effectively, my hand jostles, sending flour flying everywhere.

And I know without trying to focus on the *why* that I'm about to have company.

See, I'm really not a big fan of cops, human or supe —but that goes double when it comes to Sheriff Max Lobo. He's the head of the small law enforcement station that keeps us all in line which makes sense since that's not his only title in town.

Sheriff Lobo is also the Alpha of the Moonshadow Pack. Made up of mainly wolves (but also including ever shifter in Moonburrow), it's a heavy predator pack that is tasked with watching over the prey shifters and making sure no other supes get into trouble in town. Even if you don't respect the Alpha—and who wouldn't—you have to deal with Sheriff Lobo.

Or, if you're like me, you buy a scent-dampener charm from a coven about a half an hour away so that you can hide who and what you are from the most powerful male in town...

I've managed to do so for two months. I was planning on doing it for a lot longer if I could, but just because I'm covering up my innate *Honey*-ness, that doesn't mean that my inner opossum stops chittering whenever I sense he's near.

Or my sidekick, either.

Gus leaving tracks in the spilled flour as he races across the counter, perching near the register... yeah. He knows who's about to walk through the bakery's front door.

Considering what happened with the truth bombs this morning, so do I...

Because it's the mate who doesn't know that *I'm* his mate, and once again I'm in *trouble.*

IT COULD'VE BEEN WORSE.

Reflecting on the events of yesterday while I work out my frustrations by kneading some bread dough the next morning, I remind myself that it could've always been worse.

On the plus side, I managed to get through the conversation with Sheriff Lobo without fainting which, to me, is a huge success. He just came by because—like I'd expected, even if I hoped otherwise—the Moonburrow gossips were talking about what happened with the honesty cupcakes.

Turns out, the 'boss' that Lara mentioned is actually the mongoose mayor of Moonburrow (say *that* three times fast) and Mayor Rhimes wasn't too happy to hear that his assistant had used magic to curse his printer. The fox shifter, I learned, is Frannie, the owner of a pricy salon in town. Embarrassed by her own admission that she dyed her fur, she spilled Lara's secret to hide hers and... yeah. No surprise, it got back to the sheriff after he had to break up a witch-shifter fight that left Lara nursing a couple of scratches and Frannie cursed to be bald.

Somehow, that led to the sheriff—and the Alpha—getting involved, but since I don't shy away from the fact that this is a witch-owned bakery that sells charmed treats, I wasn't in trouble.

Small mercies, I guess. Anything that had me drawing Sheriff Lobo's attention... yeah, no. I was happy to tell him my side of the story, wave him off when he didn't push back, and hope like hell that my charm held.

For a moment there, right before he headed for the door, I wasn't so sure it did. He paused, claws tapping against the metal badge he wears pinned to his hip—the only concession that the too-handsome sheriff *is* the town sheriff—as he tilted his head just enough to sample the air. First with his open mouth, tasting the air on his tongue. Then, drawing in a deep breath before shuddering it out again.

I nearly stopped breathing myself.

He didn't say anything, though. Wearing a puzzled expression and a scowl, the sheriff let himself out of

Dough You Believe in Magic, and I refrained from having a panic attack until the lingering pine scent was as much a ghost as my prospective mate bond.

Hey. Fake it 'til you mate it, right?

Or, if you're a wound-up opossum who trembles every time you think of the predator that Fate wants to give you to, *not*.

You see, discovering that the all-power wolf shifter is my mate was the *biggest* shock to hit me once I finished relocating to Moonburrow. For the opossum who spent all of her twenty-eight years alone, never really too fussed with finding her mate just yet, the heat flooding through me when Sheriff Lobo's scent reached me fully triggered my fight or flight instincts.

Well, no. I'm a particular type of prey shifter. I have a flight or faint—or 'play dead'—response, and I was stunned when I didn't drop... even if I did do everything possible to hide myself from the sheriff's own sniffer while I figured out what the hell I was supposed to do.

I've ran into Sheriff Lobo countless times over the last two months—and, okay, it's not countless because my inner opossum has been keeping track and it's been *sixteen* times—but as far as he's concerned, I'm just the witch granddaughter of the witch baker who makes treats for his town.

And, for now, that's all I can be.

CHAPTER 3
ARE YOU SURE?

If I thought that yesterday's minor disaster meant that Dough You Believe in Magic would be a ghost town, I would be *wrong*. I should've known better. This is a supe town, after all, run by shifters with more than a few witches. I sell charmed cupcakes proudly. Something like that was bound to happen, even if it was embarrassing that it wasn't on purpose.

In fact, I had more than a few customers come in to see if there was a new batch of honesty cupcakes for them to buy. I had to refuse them all with a sorry shake of my head. I could just see it now. Unsuspecting supes being charmed into telling the truth—telling *secrets*—would definitely bring the sheriff back to my door.

Uh-uh.

No, thanks.

I did, however, guess something like that would happen. Following another one of Grandma Jean's recipes, I made Lift You Up Meringues. Delightful little pillows with a tart cherry taste, one of the meringues promised a whole hour of a great mood with no crash afterward.

I sold out of them by ten, and started pushing the almond croissants I made just in case Roxy came by. There was no sign of her, but we definitely didn't lack for customers.

It finally starts to slow around two. Taking advantage of having the store empty for a few minutes, I scarf down a magic-free danish, chase it with two slices of sourdough with my namesake smeared between the thick slabs of bread, before grabbing a lemonade from the small fridge I keep for personal use.

I'm just re-capping the bottle when the doorbell jingles, announcing a new customer.

And I do mean *new*. Around my age or maybe a few years older, it's a female shifter that I've never met before. She has dark hair cut in a fetching bob, a flatter nose with wide-set eyes… and they're pink. She has *pink* eyes.

I don't know who she is, but at least I know *what* she is.

I give her my customer service smile. "Welcome to Dough You Believe in Magic. What can I do for you?"

She doesn't quite hop, though there's undeniably a bounce to the way she walks over to me, a grin splitting her pretty face.

"Hi. I'm Betsy."

Betsy the bunny shifter. How cute. "Honey, hi."

She waves her hand, brushing away my introduction. "Oh, I know who you are. Everyone in Moonburrow knows that you're Jeannette Douce's granddaughter."

Jeannette… Grandma Jean. I nod.

"You've been the talk of Moonburrow since you arrived, and I'm sorry that it's taken me this long to visit. Your grandmother made the most divine carrot cakes. If you added that to your repertoire, I'd stop by more."

Something… probably my opossum's instincts that I should probably listen to more than I do… tells me that I might 'forget' to look for that recipe in Grandma Jean's recipe book for a while—a suspicion that is only proven to be more true when Betsy leans her elbows on the countertop, smiling up at me.

"So... I heard you spent some time with Sheriff Lobo yesterday."

I nearly choke on her casual statement. Deny, Honey. Deny deny *deny*. "What? Where did you... I don't know what you're talking about."

She lifts her eyebrows. "Hm. Maybe you need one of those honesty cupcakes that had Frannie admitting she doctors up her tail." Leaning in, the bunny confesses, "We all knew it, but none of us had the heart to point it out whenever she'd boast about it. They say foxes are sly, but in my experience, they're very insecure."

And bunnies, I'm betting, are part of the gossip circle in Moonburrow.

When I don't say anything about my unfortunate customer from yesterday, Betsy looks at me curiously. "What about you?"

I go still. Don't faint, Honey. I've been so good. I haven't dropped since I've been in Moonburrow, though the first time I caught Sheriff Lobo's scent and realized what exactly that *meant* had me touch and go for a while there. I don't want to faint now all because a curious bunny is sticking her wiggly nose in where it doesn't belong.

"What about me?"

Her pink eyes darken slightly. "You're a witch, sure, but there's something else there... something... I don't mean to offend or nothing, but a little *musky*."

Huh. I know my scent-dampener is geared specifically to a wolf's nose—especially an Alpha's sniffer—but I didn't expect any other shifter to pick up on my true supe side. Unless they spend time around opossum clans, the purple eyes might not tip 'em off… but Betsy isn't wrong. Opossums have a musk—and I have an excuse.

I click my tongue, catching Gus's attention. He lifts his head from where he was—you guessed it—fast asleep. Tapping my fingers against the counter has my sidekick getting up slowly, stretching his oversized body, and doing that strange half-run, half-gallop that belongs to us opossums.

"This is Gus," I say solemnly. "He manages Dough You Believe in Magic. I just bake here."

Betsy's mouth opens slightly, taking in the wild opossum. A second later, she giggles, and I relax.

"Well, that would explain the scent," she says. "Sorry. I heard you were a prey shifter, like me. Like so much of the town. Sheriff Lobo is a good male, but he's a wolf. A predator. If he was sniffing around the new female in town, I thought I'd stop by, introduce myself, and see if you're alright."

Pointedly ignoring how she told me that the gossips have been musing about me and my heritage, I nervously adjust the spacing between the remaining pumpkin muffins I have, then say, "Why wouldn't I be?"

She gives me a look like she thinks my head is stuffed with cotton candy instead of brains. "Because he's the top predator." Glancing over her shoulder, checking to make sure that the sheriff didn't suddenly appear while she was talking, she adds in a stage-whisper, "The *Alpha*."

Thanks, Betsy. I had no idea.

"He seems nice enough," I murmur.

Betsy snorts softly. "For a wolf, maybe. But if you get caught in his sight, watch out, that's all I'm going to say."

I give her a thin-lipped smile. "Thanks."

I guess.

Maybe.

"Well, that's that then," she chirps, oblivious to my discomfort. "I just wanted to stop by and welcome you to Moonburrow! I work at the newspaper, so if you ever want to post an ad for your bakery, you let me know. Oh! I almost forgot. We also have our prey circle meetings at the community center every other Monday evening."

I blink. Shifters aren't really religious; at least, not like humans are. We're devoted to our own gods and goddesses. For the wolves, it's their moon goddess, the Luna. For opossums, we put all our trust in Fate and Luck.

I try not to think about how bad my luck's been lately ever since I turned my back on accepting my fated mate. Then again, my quarter of witch blood could be to blame for how often I get myself into trouble since, well, I've always been a bit of a trouble-maker, on purpose or not...

Even so, I wrinkle my nose. "Prayer circle?"

Betsy shakes her head. "No. *Prey* circle. Where we share snacks and safety tips and sometimes even swap stories about what it's like to date predators."

I blink. "That's... oddly specific."

"And helpful," she adds. "Even if you're a full-blooded witch, compared to the wolves in the pack, you're one of us. Stop by on Monday." Her expression turns coy. "If you really do have Sheriff Lobo's atten-tion, who knows? You might appreciate some tips."

If I have Sheriff Lobo's attention, I'll keel over the moment he figures out that he's stuck with a prey shifter as a fated mate.

I open my mouth to give her some non-committal response while knowing that I have no intention of ever joining their prey circle, but before I can, the bell above the door chimes again.

And I freeze.

There's a wolf stalking into the bakery. Not *my* wolf. Not the one my traitorous instincts scream 'mate' at constantly, but definitely one with sharp senses and even sharper teeth.

He's good-looking. I might be biased, but most of the wolves I've met are. There's something way too tempting about such a fierce predator regardless of the fact that one growl will have me flat on my back in an instant—and I don't mean prepared to mate. I'll be 'dead', and have a whole lot of explaining to do.

In Moonburrow, I've had to get used to predators lurking everywhere. The Moonshadow Pack runs the town so it's no surprise they're always on patrol. And when they're on patrol, they're bound to get hungry.

This wolf has the usual golden eyes, only a lighter shade than Sheriff Lobo's. His hair is a lighter brown, too, with a smattering of freckles dotting his almost pretty face.

Sheriff Lobo isn't pretty. He's rugged and sexy and... and if I really want to convince myself that he can't be my mate, I need to stop comparing every male I meet in Moonburrow to its sheriff.

Betsy steps away from the counter as the wolf approaches it. True to her prey nature, she gives him a wide berth even as she says, "Hey, Declan."

He nods at her. "Stopping by for a snack, Bets?"

Her eyes go wide. "Oh. Um—"

I grab a small brown paper bag, shoving in the closest thing I can reach from the display case. "Here, Betsy. I almost forgot to give you your order."

She throws me a look of pure relief. I shrug. Whether I'm hiding what I am or not, us prey shifters have to stick together.

Betsy takes the bag from my hand, careful not to

get too close to the wolf, Declan. Once she cradles it to her chest, she waves in thanks, then bolts to the door.

One last chirp from Betsy—"Bye, Honey!"—and the bunny goes hopping away, leaving me and one of Moonburrow's big, bad wolves all alone.

Too bad it's not the one the other half of my soul is interested in... though from the way his lips quirk, revealing the points of his canines, I'm not so sure that I can't say the same for *this* wolf.

"Honey? Is that your name or do you and Betsy have something going on?"

Not that it would be any of his business if we did, but— "It's my name."

"Pretty name."

I shrug. "I've always liked it."

Grandma Jean suggested the name. She saw the patch of golden blonde hair that I was born with and, a baker through and through, gave me a name from one of the most used items in her pantry. Since Mom was too picky to come up with a name on her own, and Dad's laidback enough that he just wanted a healthy pup, Grandma Jean won out and my honest-to-Fate's name was given as Honey.

Declan offers me a crooked grin. "Pretty girl, too."

My stomach lurches. Ugh. True, I'm unmated at the moment, but tell that to my inner opossum screeching that this wolf is *not* my mate and shouldn't be hitting on me like this unless he wants his Alpha to show him what his intestines look like—

And, yup, that right there is why I can't let the sheriff know what I know until I'm one hundred percent sure I can handle a predator.

Since I can't, and rejecting the wolf in front of me might be just as bad as losing control and throwing a day-old roll in his face, I move away from the bread and closer to the register.

"What can I get for you?"

The pleasant tone combined with the earnest yet clear 'not interested' smile does its job. He chuckles under his breath, realizing that his smooth moves won't work on me, then casts his gaze over the display case.

"I don't know. It all looks so delicious. What do you suggest?"

All of it because I put love, sweat, and sugar into every morsel?

"The scones are pretty good. Oh, I sell a ton of these cheese danishes. The cherry hand pies. I have croissants, almond, chocolate, and plain. Any of that sound good to you?"

"Sounds perfect. I'll take ten."

I blink. Lounging on his flour throne, Gus lifts his head, sensing my confusion. He turns his beady gaze on Declan, decides he's just a customer, and instead of moving to stand next to me like he did when the sheriff was here, he goes right back to sleep.

Lucky.

Declan is waiting for me to stay something.

Right.

"Um. Okay. Ten of which one exactly?"

"All of the ones you mentioned."

Oh. "That will be sixty baked goods."

Declan pulls his wallet out of his back pocket. "That's right. You take card?"

I bob my head, a stunned nod. Sixty items in one go that's not a catering order is new for me. "Yeah, but—"

He tosses a card onto the counter. "We're having a pack council meeting tonight. At least fifteen wolves will be there. Now that I think of it, can we add a cake? You do cakes, right?"

"I have a vanilla chiffon cake in the back fridge and a chocolate cake, too—"

He laughs, the sound more like a bark than anything else since there isn't actually any humor in it. "No chocolate, thanks. Us wolves can eat a lot, but that stuff doesn't sit well."

Right. Because chocolate is poisonous to dogs, and wolves are basically just a pup's wild ancestor. "So the vanilla chiffon?"

"And the rest of what you suggested."

Okay.

I plug the order into the register before I forget, then disappear into the back to grab the vanilla chiffon cake from the fridge. I'd planned on putting slices out for tomorrow's sample, but if Declan wants to buy it along with half my remaining stock, I'm not going to stop him.

Though, as I open the fridge and see the smaller white box on the shelf above the cake, I pause.

Should I...

I don't know...

Screw it.

I grab the cake box, add the smaller box on top of it, close the fridge door with my hip, and head back out into the bakery.

At the counter, I set the stack down, moving the small box to the side. After that, I get down to business while Declan makes small talk that I'm barely paying attention to. I don't want to lose count as I start loading up boxes and bags with his order, though I'm pretty sure I did. Ah, well. As long as I gave him a couple of extras instead of cheating him, that's fine.

Once I'm done, I move the cake to the counter, followed by the pastry boxes, plus three separate bags of croissants. I tally up his order, slightly impressed when he doesn't even bat an eye when I give him his total, then run his card through my reader.

"It go through?" he asks.

Since the receipt is printing, I nod. "Yes."

"Pack credit card. Don't leave home without it."

He grins. I hand him the card and the credit slip to sign, which he does with a sguiggle and a flourish before he tucks the card back into his wallet.

I gesture at the array of baked goods. "Would you like some help?"

"Nah. I've got a car outside. I've got it."

"If you're sure..."

He winks at me. "I'm a wolf, sweetness. Don't you worry about me."

Honey, I want to snap. My name is Honey.

But I don't. Instead, I reach for the smaller white box.

"What about this? Do you think you can take that, too?"

His eyes light up. "That for me?"

Um. No. "Actually, if you're going to a pack council meeting tonight... I'm assuming the sheriff will be there?"

"He is the Alpha."

Don't I know it?

"Could you give this to him? From me?"

For a moment, Declan's easygoing grin lingers—but only for a moment before it's replaced by a genuine look of surprise. "Are *you* sure about that? Giving food to the Alpha?"

Good question.

To tell the truth, I've been puzzled by this particular cupcake all day, and handing it over to the wolf doesn't change that one bit.

It's supposed to be a peace offering, the only way I know how to make one these days. I managed to apologize to my customers yesterday by offering them free eclairs before shooing them out my door, but I was so flustered the entire time Sheriff Lobo was in the bakery, I didn't offer him a single pastry as an apology for involving him in my boo-boo.

It hit me this morning that I didn't. Before I knew better, I whipped up a charm-free cupcake with apples and caramel because... I don't know... he just seemed like that kind of male. If he didn't want it, he didn't have to eat it, but I'd be lying if I said that I... I kind of want him to.

And that, right there, is a big fucking problem.

In shifter culture, food has meaning. If you feed someone unmated that you could potentially be attracted to, it's not just a meal. It's telling them that you are a provider, that they'll never go hungry or want for anything if you're around. If I was a predator, giving the sheriff a cupcake now would be like I was trying to feed him.

I'd be giving him a sign that I was into him as a mate.

Now, I've only been in Moonburrow for two months, but I've dealt with my fair share of predators. He's the *Alpha*. He'd never want a prey shifter for a mate, and, yeah, that's what I am. A prey shifter feeding a predator is kind of just doing their job, showing respect, so I'm not too worried about Sheriff Lobo getting the wrong idea.

I'm the baker, after all. Giving away treats is what I do.

When it comes to the sheriff, it's all I *can* do.

I can't have him. Mixed shifter matings—predator and prey—only work when they trust each other enough to form and finalize a mate bond. How? Predators either want to protect or pounce while prey just want to submit or flee. It'll never work, and I have no clue what Fate is thinking, telling me that I'm meant for the sheriff... even if the handful of minutes I spent in close proximity with him last night only reaffirmed what I suspected the first time I picked up his scent.

I'm supposed to be his mate, and since that's not going to happen, the least I can do is apologize with a cupcake.

"Yeah," I tell Declan. "I'm sure."

CHAPTER 4
PEPPERMINT

After a long day on my feet, I'm exhausted and ready to go upstairs to relax for the evening. It's almost time. We're... or, really, *I* since Gus is curled up around a cake stand on the counter, snuffling as he sleeps... prepped for tomorrow morning. The leftover goods that haven't been sold have been bagged up and set aside for drop-off at the Moonburrow food bank for donation; considering how much shifters eat—especially the predators—there's always someone in need, even in a shifter town that relies on pack and community more than humans do in their suburbs and cities. It's my way to help, and if it's not something I can repurpose or sell as day-old, it goes to supes who will happily gobble up my treats. The day's receipts have been reconciled, too, the deposit tucked in the safe. I'll drop the money off, plus the donation during my mid-morning break tomorrow before heading back to prep for the lunch rush.

But that's all tomorrow. Tonight? I'm going to take a shower, throw on some comfy PJs, pick a movie to watch, and zone out with the frozen pizza that's been calling my name for the last hour or so.

Sounds like a plan. I just need to grab Gus and—

Gus.

Where's Gus?

Two seconds ago, he was zonked-out, his reflection in the cake stand leaving two slumbering opossums on the countertop. Now? There isn't a single one. No large opossum with his coarse whitish-grey fur and adorable ears. Not on the flour bag he claimed my first morning in the bakery, or searching determinedly for any few stray crumbs he won't be able to find in the freshly cleaned display case.

"Gus?" I call out. "Where are you, bud?"

Over the slight hum from the lights, I hear a familiar sound coming from the back. It's mainly the kitchen with my industrial mixers, multiple ovens, and cooling racks, but at the end of the space, there's an exit that leads out into the back alley where we have our dumpster.

That's where I find him. Standing in front of the door, his hackles raised and his tail lashing, Gus hisses at it.

"What's wrong?"

His beady eyes focus on the back door for a split second longer before he turns toward me as though he can't help himself. After closing the gap between us with his adorable little shuffle, Gus climbs up my leg, my side, my shoulder. He settles there, wrapping his prehensile tail around my throat.

I wait for him to make some kind of sound that might help me understand what upset him, but all he does is nuzzle close to my skin.

I pat his head. "Alright, buddy. Let's go upstairs. We have an early morning tomorrow."

Hell, I run my own bakery. I have an early morning *every* morning—except for Mondays 'cause we're off, but still. If there's something skulking around the back alley behind the bakery, it can wait until tomorrow.

Who knows? It's probably just Roxy, smirking as she realized that I went to a local hardware shop and convinced the shy if knowledgeable mole shifter owner to teach me how to change the lock on my back door before she can break in to the bakery again.

I smile to myself as I scratch Gus under his chin, flicking off the main lights to the bakery.

That trip took almost an hour before dinner yesterday, plus the twenty bucks it cost for the supplies. When I see the look on Roxy's face the next time she tries to pilfer some pastries, it'll be worth it.

Hey. She grew up, but so did I. And while we might be friends-ish these days, I'm not the pushover I used to be—

Gus makes a mild clicking sound.

I cock my head. "Mm? What's that?"

The clicks become an insistent chittering.

"Okay. If you want eggs for dinner, you can have eggs."

He rubs the edge of his bare, scaly, pink opossum tail against my throat, Gus's version of a *thanks*.

Okay. I'm not a pushover to anyone except Gus, that is.

That's okay. He's worth it.

And even if he wasn't, from the moment he imprinted on me as a young opossum seeing me while I was in my fur, he's been my loyal sidekick, my best buddy, and the only roommate I've had and... wow.

Maybe I do need to get out more.

Prey circle, huh? Well. Maybe I should never say never.

It's five o'clock in the morning when Gus and I head downstairs to start our day.

Ah. The life of a baker.

Opossums in the wild are nocturnal. They also have a lifespan of about two years or so; four in captivity. Most of my witchy side is only really good for following Grandma Jean's recipes. I can't cast any spells, not even simple ones like my mom can. Still, maybe there's something magical about me since I've already had Gus as my sidekick for *eight* years and he shows no sign of slowing down. Plus, he keeps to my hours, and if that's not magical, I don't know what is.

I found him hiding behind a trash can when I was working in a coffee shop back in Glenville. He'd been much smaller than—he's about the size of a house cat now—and all alone. He hissed at me, but when I quickly shucked off my clothes, shifting to my fur, the abandoned opossum immediately latched onto me.

And I mean that *literally*. Gus didn't crawl into my pouch... and, no, it's not weird that I have a pouch when I'm my opossum since I *am* a marsupial, after all... but he did scurry up on my back, holding on tightly.

From then on, it's been the two of us. Honey and Gus, and he doesn't mind that I spend most of my time in my skin. The big human feeds him, brushes him, and makes sure he doesn't get the stray tick on him... of course we're buddies.

He's riding my shoulder now. As soon as we reach the bottom of the steps and I push open the door that separates the kitchen from the stairs that lead up to the apartment built over the shop, he digs his teensy claws through my oversized pink sweater, finding enough skin that I yip.

"Gus? What's the matter?"

He curls his tail around the back of my neck, burying his face in the side.

I pat his flank. "I know. It's early. Why don't you get comfy while I get to work?"

I move us from the kitchen to the store space, resting my hand on the back counter. Gus meanders his way down my arm, plopping on the counter, whiskers twitching. His corner has a brown basket with a fuzzy tan blanket in it. He's slept in it maybe twice in the last two months, preferring the ten-pound bag of flour that I'd knocked onto its side once before Gus claimed it as his throne.

Mimicking me when I knead dough, he's done the opossum version of cat biscuits, making the hard sack comfortable without tearing open the thick paper on the bag. Gus sniffs the flour, declares it acceptable, and curls up on top of it.

I playfully tweak one of his pink ears, then get started on my morning prep.

There's so much to do and, after rolling up my sleeves, I get down to it. Proofing dough, getting batter ready, checking on the puff pastry that chilled overnight... I'm working as the sun comes up, streaking in through the large bakery windows. Despite so many shifters in Moonburrow, this part of the town is definitely diurnal. If I thought I could get away with having a nighttime bakery, I would've changed the hours, but since Grandma Jean was used to human hours—and so was I after spending so long in Glenville—I kept them the same.

That means that I'm up at four a.m., down at the bakery by five, and in bed by nine at the latest. I spend a lot of time with just me and Gus, and I don't mind it. No. I'm not lonely. No. I'm not wondering what Max Lobo is doing right now...

Nope. That way lies danger, and instead of letting my mind wander, I change the trash bag out. I'd filled it up during prep this morning, and I prefer keeping it empty unless it's too busy for me to rush outside to toss it in the dumpster.

Just as I'm knotting the big, black trash bag together so that it doesn't spill, Gus perks up his head. He sees the trash bag, clicks his teeth, and stretches. Before I can even start for the swinging door that leads to the kitchen, he's at my heels, chittering in his way at me to hurry up.

I heft up the bag, peering down at Gus.

"You my little guard opossum this morning? Okay. Come along."

He doesn't often join me on my early morning trash runs, but something's been worrying Gus since last night. Maybe I'm ridiculous. It's more than likely. Still, I trust his wild opossum instincts way more than my coddled inner beast. If he thinks something's up, I don't mind following him out back into the alley that houses the dumpster.

The moment I unlock the back door and step outside, I shift the weight of the trash bag, using my free hand to cover my nose.

Woof. It smells like a candy cane factory blew up back here. Peppermint overwhelms everything, and considering the dumpster is only emptied once a week and the trash tends to stink even though it's mid-autumn, that's a mighty impressive feat. I'm an opossum shifter and it completely blows out my nose.

At my feet, Gus is pawing his snout. He doesn't like it, either.

I use my elbow to gesture behind me. The door's still open. My voice comes out muffled, thanks to the way I'm pinching my nose. "Go back in, bud. You don't have to smell this."

Gus stops pawing his face, the pointed look in his beady black eyes telling me that, if I'm going to drop off the trash, he's coming with me.

Fine. Let's get this over with.

The peppermint is giving me a headache. I march over to the dumpster, tossing the trash bag inside of it.

There. I turn, ready to head back in—and that's when I notice a pair of legs... boots... *something* sticking out from the other side of the dumpster.

My initial impression is that someone is sitting up against the metal side, kicking their legs out. The shadow makes the fabric look dark. Black, perhaps?

"Roxy? If you're pissed that I changed the lock on the back door and that meant you couldn't break in, you don't have to sit on the nasty asphalt and pout about it. All you had to do was knock at the front. I have some leftover almond croissants I saved for you."

Huh. No answer.

So either Roxy really is pissed, she's fucking with me, or... or that's not Roxy.

I should go back inside. It stinks like Christmas in early November, my eyes are watering, and Gus is now pawing at my ankle, his tiny claws snagging on the fabric of my legging. Something's not right, but I'm also not about to leave someone sitting in the alley when I can help them.

"Rox? Is that you?"

Still no answer.

Wiping my nervous hands on my thighs, I take a few steps and peer around the side of the dumpster.

It's not Roxy.

It's...

It's...

It's Declan, the wolf who made up the bulk of my sales yesterday.

And he's *dead.*

There's no denying it. Those are his dark blue jeans and his dark boots sticking out, connected to a male body crumpled on his side. His tan skin had faded to a waxy white. His face is halfway transformed; his nose is a muzzle, and his teeth are fangs. His lips are a deep blue. His eyes, open and wide and staring, are *silver.*

His hand is outstretched. In the few seconds that I catalog the scene, I notice that. He might have been sitting up against the dumpster, or maybe he was tossed behind it like trash, but before he died, he'd had one last treat.

Because there, mere inches away from his outstretched hand, is the cupcake I gave him yesterday. The fried apple and caramel confection I made specifically for Sheriff Lobo, that Declan said he'd bring to the Alpha... I don't need my own snout to smell it. I know by sight that the cupcake is mine, as is the small white box stamped with Dough You Believe in Magic's logo on the top.

The cupcake is missing one bite. A single bite. The near-miniscule smear of light brown frosting stands out against his blue lips. It's the same frosting as on the cupcake leaving no doubt that Declan ate the magic-free cupcake I made for Sheriff Lobo.

And then, somehow, he died.

He died.

He's *dead*, and as the light-headedness in my brain gives way to complete unconsciousness, I just hope that I don't crack my skull on the asphalt as I drop.

THERE ARE ACCEPTABLE REASONS TO BE IN AN ALLEY AT dawn. Finding a body is not one of them.

It's even worse when you're an opossum shifter who 'died' yourself upon realizing that there's a dead predator at your door, and that the only thing that you remember seeing next to him is a cupcake from your bakery missing a single bite.

But you know what's the real cherry on the top of the crap sundae? Is when you finally come to again, you find two very imposing figures crouched down next to you.

Each male is wearing a cloth mask, protecting their mouths and their noses from the peppermint stink that's only gotten worse since I fainted. Even so, a very prominent part of me catches a hint of pine and, even half-conscious, I know exactly who one of them is.

Which is precisely why I focus on the other.

He's huge. I'd guess he'd be tall when he was on his feet, but this male has a broad build with shoulders that might be too wide to fit through my back door. His eyes are gun-metal grey, his dark hair slicked back off of a deeply tanned face. His muscles have muscles, and if he clamped his massive hands over my head, he could screw it off my neck like it was a bottle cap.

If that gives the impression that he's a thug, that couldn't be more wrong. His silk shirt molds to his chest perfectly, the color an exact match to his eyes. This close, I can tell he's wearing a pair of impeccably tailored dark grey trousers. He looks like he belongs in a villa in Italy, not in Moonburrow.

He doesn't say anything, not even when it becomes obvious that I'm both a) not dead, and b) finally conscious again. On the plus side, they left me where I fell instead of shipping me off to the Moonburrow morgue... assuming we *have* one... and the reassuring weight of Gus resting on one of my custom braids tells me that my opossum hadn't left my side while I was 'dead'.

He shifts closer, humming against my neck as the big guy to my left turns to look at his companion.

Ah, crud. That means I should, too.

Swallowing the nervous lump in my throat, I force myself to meet his golden gaze and hope that I don't faint again.

CHAPTER 5
INTERROGATION

Sheriff Max Lobo. He has rich russet-colored hair, leaning toward making him more of a brunet, that's slightly long in the front; I have to curl my fingers at my side to resist the urge to see if it's as soft as it looks. I already know the rugged, handsome features that are currently covered up by the mask, though I can imagine his jaw is clenched tight as he waits for me to... what?

Explain myself?

Get off the ground?

Blurt out a confession that I killed Declan?

Declan… the way they're crouched around me, I can't see the dead wolf. I do, however, notice that there are at least four other Moonshadow wolves gathered around the spot where the body fell. They also have masks, except for one who is pinching his nose and shaking his head.

They're probably searching for some sort of scent trail. Either to understand what happened to Declan or to gauge whether anyone else was near here when he died. There's no fucking way that my cupcake had anything to do with it—it was a basic recipe, not a drop of magic added—but the way these two wolves are watching me… I'm beginning to understand just how suspicious this looks.

I can only imagine what happened when Sheriff Lobo and the other wolves were alerted to the scene, even if I have no idea how that happened or how long I was out for. They probably thought me and Declan both had been murdered, but while humans are simple enough to think a missing pulse equals a dead girl, I figure a wolf shifter would realize fairly quickly I was actually just catatonic.

So they waited for me to wake up, and now I have, and the only thing on my mind is confessing to my fated mate that I'm innocent so that he can go away and leave me alone.

"I didn't do it," I blurt out.

The big male glances at Sheriff Lobo.

The sheriff reaches out, gripping my eyelid. It takes everything I have not to tremble when he makes contact with me for the first time, but all he does is peer into my eyes, checking for a concussion or something.

Gus moves until he's sitting on my chest.

The big guy reaches for him.

I hurriedly sit up, cradling Gus close—and knocking the sheriff away. "No. I mean it. Gus and me... this is Gus, by the way... we were just throwing out trash this morning before opening when we found the dead predator."

"Wolf," rumbles Sheriff Lobo.

Um. Okay.

"That's Declan Rowe," he continues. "He was a delta in the Moonshadow Pack and someone killed him on your territory. There was a report that there were two bodies here. My deputy and I came with our team... and here you are. Very much alive. And my wolf... he seems to not be after eating one of your tainted cupcakes."

Well. No way I can deny any of that, can I? Not when he put it so succinctly.

You know what? That's just my luck.

Of course the sheriff had to find my supposedly dead body next to a corpse. Especially after he already had to come to Dough You Believe in Magic and scold me over the honesty cupcake fiasco.

"My cupcakes aren't stained! And I don't know who he is." Well, no. That's not quite true. "I mean, I only met him yesterday. He said his name was Declan when he bought a whole ton of baked goods from me, but I don't know what he'd be doing out here with that!"

"Did you give it to him?"

Shit. "Well, yes—"

His eyes flash. "To poison him?"

What? "No! He wasn't supposed to eat it. *You* were."

Oh, you've got to be kidding me. I'm never my best when I'm coming out of a faint—claiming it's narcolepsy isn't too far off—but you think I would've thought twice before I blurted *that* out.

The other male goes very, very still. "Are you telling me that your target was the Alpha?"

If I drop again, I wouldn't be surprised. The air is thick with danger, hormones, and dominance, and I'm not sure who is wearing it more: the sheriff or his deputy.

"I didn't target anyone! I'm just a baker!"

"So you say. Tell me, Ms. Morgan—"

"Honey." It squeaks out. "My name is Honey."

Up until yesterday, I was fine with having him call me Ms. Morgan. He's Sheriff Lobo. I'm good with keeping the distance. But if he really thinks that I have anything to do with this, I need him to see *Honey.*

His brow furrows. "Honey. Do you bake with peppermint extract?"

"That's a Christmas flavor. I'm still transitioning from Halloween treats to Thanksgiving." That's true, but it takes me a second before I realize why he asked. "I didn't make it stink like this back here!"

"Whoever did knew that it would blow a wolf's nose out," mutters the big male. "Even through the mask, it's rough. Maybe we should bring her inside if you want to get her statement."

Right. Now that I'm awake, they don't see any reason to keep me out here. And if I'm gone, it might allow the other wolves to take away the body of their fallen packmate and, I don't know, search for some clues about what happened to Declan.

It has to be murder, right? It's hard enough to eliminate a shifter, but it's not like he would've killed himself. It's not how we're wired. Our protective instincts are too strong, and our regenerative properties too high. As far as I know, only two things can truly kill a shifter: a crap ton of silver and getting our heads chopped off. I think I would've noticed if Declan's head was removed from the rest of his body. It *could* be silver, but then what does one of my cupcakes have to do with it?

Why did he die outside my bakery?

I don't know, but the way the sheriff and the deputy

are watching me as though I should have all the answers, I think I better figure it out.

Stroking Gus's head, trying to calm both my opossum and, well, my opossum, I do everything I can *not* to grimace.

I moved to Moonburrow so that I could stop waking up near dead bodies.

This is *not* an improvement.

<hr>

BEING ESCORTED TO THE SHERIFF STATION WASN'T ON MY bingo card, but knowing the way that both Fate and Luck seemed to have taken a curious interest in one silly opossum's life, it should've been.

When the big male wolf suggested that they bring me inside to 'take my statement'—or, you know, interrogate me—I figured he meant that we could hustle into the bakery. I could offer snacks, maybe make some hot chocolate to settle my nerves... yeah. He had a totally different idea.

We *did* go inside, but only because the sheriff was being careful to keep Declan and his final resting spot cordoned off. The deputy murmured something to one of the other wolves, then the three of us... four, if you count Gus... entered the kitchen, started to cut through it, and paused when the scent of burnt bread and sugar slammed into us.

"My ovens!" I cried, panicking again when I saw pale grey plumes of smoke escaping at least one of them.

On the plus side, I didn't burn Dough You Believe in Magic down. Then again, considering I was unconscious for about two and a half hours according to the wall clock, I'm lucky that some charred buns and too-crispy danishes were the worst of the loss.

The bakery was still closed. Obviously. I'm open every day except for Monday, and I hated to think how many customers saw the 'closed' sign on the front door and wondered what was up since today is Friday. It'll have to stay that way a little longer, too, I thought, then unlocked the door so we could exit through the front.

The sheriff was being very careful to put a little distance between us, torn between treating me as a suspect and another possible victim, but he cleared his throat when he noticed that Gus was curled up on my shoulder, intent on joining us. Borrowing Roxy's teasing quip, I told him that Gus is my emotional support opossum, and he just nodded and instructed me to climb into the backseat of the police cruiser emblazoned with the word 'sheriff' over the much smaller 'Moonburrow' beneath it.

Turns out, I've passed the sheriff's office a couple of times without having any idea. Moonburrow is basically your idyllic supernatural town, as suburban as you can get for the most part. The pack territory expands a little further than that. When the sheriff is being the Alpha, he has a seat of power in a hundred acre wooded area where the predators live in cabin-like homes with territory to roam instead of close houses and condos where prey shifters gather, believing the old adage that there is safety in numbers.

Because Sheriff Lobo is responsible for Moonburrow as a whole, he has an Alpha cabin in the woods, plus a small office where he can hang his nonexistent hat when he's in downtown Moonburrow.

Nestled between a wolf-owned butcher shop and a laundromat, there's an unmarked door with a plane of tinted glass on each side. Sheriff Lobo pulls the cruiser in front of it, the only car parking along this pedestrian-heavy street.

I've been watching him the entire ride. You'd think his eyes would be on the road. Not even close. His predatory stare keeps flickering to the rear view mirror, watching me right back.

Once we were away from the overwhelming peppermint, both wolves removed their masks. The deputy is as classically handsome as I figured he would be, but while there is some similarity in their features, I'd be lying if I didn't say that I preferred Sheriff Lobo's.

So maybe I'm biased. That's not a bad thing. I should probably be attracted to my fated mate.

His nostrils flare. I stiffen. Here's hoping my scent-dampener charm holds or else I'll have even more problems...

I didn't kill that wolf, but someone seems to be going to a little trouble to make it appear like I did. The cupcake... I can't stop thinking about the cupcake. I made it for the sheriff... I made it for my *mate*... and there's no way I would've put anything in it that might hurt a predator.

But how do I explain that without revealing *all* of my truths?

I don't know. Luckily, I have a small reprieve as the deputy opens the back door, waiting for me to scoot my way out. By the time I'm standing, Gus chittering softly in my ear, the sheriff is gone, already stalking inside the unmarked door.

I guess I should be glad that they don't put me in cuffs. That's not how it's done in shifter communities. Silver causes too much damage, while iron and steel could barely keep a pup contained. Besides, justice is swift. If he knew for sure that I killed Declan, as the Alpha, he'd take care of it. As it is, with the peppermint extract removing his greatest asset—his sniffer—he has to rely on his 'sheriff' side to solve the crime.

And that, it seems, includes interrogating me like I thought—or, I should say, having *his* sidekick do the job since he's nowhere to be found.

The big male finally introduces himself as Riordan, Max Lobo's right-hand wolf... which, I realize an instant later, makes him the Moonshadow Pack Beta. He's also the deputy, and he leads Gus and me into a closed-off room that has a small rectangular table, four chairs, and a mirrored window that I'd bet the lease to Dough You Believe in Magic is two-way, and that Sheriff Lobo is on the other side of it right now, watching me get settled in one of the seats.

I'm nervous. Shaky. I haven't eaten yet, and I *died*. My braids are mussed. I have a smear of dirt on my cheek, my face paler than usual. The way my eyes are wide gives me a sudden stunned look. Add my opossum scarf and... yeah. I'm not too surprised when Riordan asks me if I want anything before we start.

My initial instinct is to say no. My stomach has been flip-flopping since I woke up so close to my fated mate, and the memory of Declan's blue lips will be haunting me for a while. I can sense Gus's hunger, though, and I ask mildly, "Do you have any fruit?"

Riordan glances at the mirror, already proving my suspicions right because, only a few minutes later, Sheriff Lobo walks into the room, carrying a plate of apple slices and red grapes in, plus a glass of water.

He sets them both in front of me before taking the seat opposite me. Riordan moves to the corner, crossing his arms over his broad chest, leaning up against the wall so he can leave the real interrogation to the Alpha after all.

I'm already crumbling. The peppermint blew out

my snout, too. Here, in his office, I'm wrapped up in his dark pine scent and his gleaming gold eyes.

And the food…

Ah, crud. My maybe mate is offering me food. I know he's just playing good cop after Riordan got me settled down. I know he's not propositioning me with a plate of fruit. Still, tell that to my inner opossum.

I take one of the grapes, passing it to Gus. He clicks his teeth, showing me his appreciation, then gets to work on nibbling the piece of fruit.

Leaving the rest of the plate alone for now, I take a sip from my glass of water, then give the two wolves a nervous smile.

A small notebook appears in one of Sheriff Lobo's paws, a pen in the other.

"Okay," he says, jaw flexing. Something is bothering him, too—and I almost want to slap my forehead. Murder investigation, Honey. Have you forgotten? "Why don't we start from the beginning?"

The beginning? Yeah. I can do that.

Because I haven't forgotten, and I might be new to Moonburrow, but I definitely don't want my rep to go from baker to *murderer…*

So I tell him everything; well, *almost* everything. From how Declan stopped by to buy enough treats for the pack meeting—and since both Riordan and the sheriff nodded, it seemed that was true—to me giving him the cupcake for Sheriff Lobo, and how Gus seemed perturbed last night before we went to bed, almost like he sensed someone lurking in the back alley.

I do take a moment to introduce Gus, passing him another apple slice to fill his mouth after he hops onto the tabletop, baring his fangs at the sheriff. For a second, I was sure he was going to launch himself at the wolf shifter, maybe take a bite out of him. Since that would only get me in more trouble, I bribed Gus with a snack, then continued.

I tell them both about how I went down to the bakery to start morning prep, eventually needed to toss the trash, and got my nose stuffed-up with the peppermint stink. They exchanged a look at that, then another when I got to the part of the story when I saw the boots first, the body next, then passed out.

I don't tell them that I was playing dead. I don't know how long the wolves were on the scene or how 'dead' I looked, but for anyone who isn't familiar with opossum shifters, it might look like I'm a skittish witch who simply fainted. Neither male asks me about it, though they do confirm they arrived in the alley about fifteen minutes before I came to again.

All that done, I take another sip of my water. Good thing I swallowed it before the sheriff makes his next comment or I might've ended up spitting it all over poor Gus.

"Let's talk about the cupcake."

I really don't want to talk about the cupcake. "Um. Okay."

"You said that you intended me to have it." He raises his eyebrows. "Is that true?"

Shoot me now. "Yes. But not like I was trying to poison you... I wasn't trying to poison anyone! It wasn't even a charmed cupcake," I insist because it seems important that he knows this wasn't another Can't Resist Cupcake sitch, "but just a really yummy caramel apple cupcake. It was a peace offering. To say sorry after you had to stop at the bakery when I accidentally baked honesty cupcakes."

He purses his lips. Damn it. A rugged wolf shifter in his early thirties should not look as gorgeous as Max Lobo does when he makes an expression like that. "I remember. And you're sure that wasn't another magicked cupcake?"

"Positive."

"But you're a witch."

Danger alert, Honey. *Danger.*

"So? That doesn't mean everything in my bakery has magic in it. I can barely use any at all. My best trick is knowing when the oven timer will go off ten seconds before it does and being able to measure out herbs and spices. Test the cupcake. You'll see. No magic at all."

Sheriff Lobo makes a note in his book. I'm sure he's going to do exactly that, and at least that's one way I'll be vindicated.

"Okay. Now about you, Ms. Morgan."

"Honey."

This time, he just nods. "There's something about you. I can't quite put my claw on it. My wolf keeps telling me that you're hiding something." His eyes flash again, the power of his alpha wolf in their depths. "What is it, Honey?"

It's my name. It's in the way he rasps my name.

He's an Alpha. Sure, he's the sheriff, too, but one look at Max Lobo and there's no denying how powerful his wolf is. A born alpha—his rank and hierarchy in the pack—who worked his way up to being the *Alpha*, the ruler of it. At that level, there are certain perks. Total obedience. Shifters who will bare their throat rather than challenge him. A separate bond with the Luna, the wolf shifters' goddess... and the ability to use their senses to know when a shifter under their protection is lying to them.

I can't lie. Not outright. It would be impossible to, and no matter what happens between the sheriff and me in the future, I *won't* lie. Sure, hiding things for my own safety is one thing, but the way he's watching me, his wolf expecting an answer...

Fuck it. I have to give him one.

"I *am* a witch." I sink down in my seat. "A quarter-witch, on my mom's side. Grandma Jean was full-blooded, but my grandfather wasn't."

The sheriff's brow furrows again, deeper this time. "Then what was he?"

I gulp. "A shifter."

Poor male. He looks like he's barely resisting the urge to climb across the table and throttle me for just admitting this now. What makes it even worse is that I'm used to getting such a look from other shifters, both predators and prey.

"Okay. What kind of shifter?"

I hesitate.

Riordan pushes up from his lean, stalking closer to the table. "You should tell him."

I know I should. He's the sheriff, I'm a murder suspect, but none of that compares to the reality that I'm also his mate. I *should* tell him, and I do.

"Opossum."

CHAPTER 6
VIRGINIA OPOSSUM

Burp.

Okay. Maybe this wolf isn't so bad.

— GUS

Silence. Pure, unadulterated *silence*.

Yeah. I'd been expecting that.

Outside of Onancock, it's not as common to find prey shifters unless we're in a sanctuary city. It's a safety thing; our safety, and the safety of keeping the supernatural world a secret. When the clan knows to protect a fallen opossum, we're nowhere near as vulnerable as a headstrong ding-dong who decided she'd move to a human town and found herself waking up in the morgue not once, not twice, but *three* times…

"That's what happened in the back alley," I blurt out, figuring: in for a penny, in for a pound. I might as well explain myself now that he knows the truth. "Yeah, I fainted, but not because I'm some kind of frightened witch. It was more of a genetic disposition, the same way wolf shifters can't help but howl at the moon, you know?"

The sheriff opens his mouth once, thinks better of what he's about to say, then lets it shut with a near-audible *click*. A muscle tics in his cheek. He frowns.

I give him a tiny smile.

"You're a—" He stops again. The frown deepens. "You shift into a... possum? I have that right?"

"Opossum," I correct. Sorry. It's habit. "With an 'o'."

"But... and I just want to make this clear... you're a prey shifter?"

Ah, crud. I see where this is going—and, if I'm right, it has nothing to do with his position as sheriff of Moonburrow.

Oh, no. This is all about Max Lobo being the Alpha of the Moonshadow Pack.

"Um. Yes."

"And you understand that all shifters in Moonburrow are, by default, members of my pack?"

Damn it. "Uh-huh."

"And that, as the only opossum shifter I'm aware of in town, it can be dangerous if you appear as dead as you did earlier today? Because I'll be honest with you:

Riordan was almost sure you *did* die, just like Declan. Right?"

The Beta nods. "I couldn't smell you, but I couldn't hear your heartbeat, either. How did you do that?"

"I was startled when I saw the dead predator. I reacted. I *am* an opossum, and that means I might have engaged in... defensive stillness."

"You played dead."

"I played dead," I say, agreeing with Riordan.

The sheriff has stayed quiet for the exchange—and that's when the strangest thing happens. For a moment, he just stares at me. I know I'm dealing with the Alpha right now, but maybe I do have a death wish of my own because I sneak a peek at his eyes. I'm careful; it's nowhere long enough for the powerful Alpha to take the eye contact as a challenge from the prey shifter a head shorter than him. Still, I look, and my stomach goes tight.

His expression, from the taut lines bracketing his full lips to the way his gold-colored eyes focus on me unblinkingly, is a mixture of surprise and concern. Almost like he's realizing that the universe just plopped an anxious marsupial with a tendency to play dead into his lap that he's now responsible to protect— and that's assuming he doesn't book me for murder first.

I could deal with that. Back in Onancock, our pack was made up of mainly prey shifters, but even we knew better than to hide completely from predators. We needed a handful to keep us out of trouble, and mountain lion shifter Colin Woodrow did his best without losing his temper too often. Having a powerful Alpha look at me like I was nothing but trouble... I could deal with that.

But when the sheriff's wolf eyes soften just enough to tell me that his beast seems almost *pleased* at the idea that he's now—according to shifter politics—responsible for me like the rest of the shifters in Moonburrow... I almost want to shift and hide under the table to escape the way he's suddenly looking at me.

My charm should still be holding. I have to reapply the scent-dampener potion every morning, and I did this one. If he had to ask what I am, he can't scent me so that means he has no idea that I'm his mate. This is just his overprotective Alpha instincts at work, especially since he's dealing with the death of one of his packmates.

That's the most important part. Finding out what happened to Declan. For the moment, it seems like I'm still being treated as both suspect and victim. Riordan eventually tells me I'm free to go, but that I shouldn't make any plans to leave Moonburrow. The sheriff himself walks me out the door, and if my inner opossum is going nuts being this close to him, I do my best to pretend like he's not affecting me one bit.

Gus is curled up in my arms, halfway dazed in a

fruit coma. He does slap at Sheriff Lobo with the tip of his tail, but I hurriedly tuck that part of him under my hand before the wolf shifter can growl at my opossum.

He seems even more curious about my sidekick now, though I can... I don't know, *sense* it versus it having anything to do with what he's saying with actual words.

I don't completely explain Gus. It's bad enough I had to confess my prey nature. I might not be able to protect myself, but when it comes to my sidekick, I can be as fierce as any predator.

As though he can tell, he keeps any comments to himself. He's a scowly, intimidating sheriff, and if I have to work hard not to scoot up his behind because he radiates 'safety' in a way that amazes me, I do it.

He offers to give me a ride home. I quickly decline. The idea of being in a car with just me, Gus, and the sheriff... his scent enveloping me... nowhere to run? No. Not a good idea. Besides, it's barely a twenty-minute walk back to the bakery. I'm fine.

I'm just about to shove the door open and make my escape when he murmurs my name softly. "Honey?"

My heart lodges in my throat. Don't faint, Honey, don't faint... "Yes?"

Sheriff Lobo hands me a small, white rectangle. "Here's my card. Call if anything scares you again. Either of you."

I take the card, but my pride has me tilting my chin

up. I don't meet his eyes again—I'm not suicidal enough to engage in another daring stare with an alpha predator—though I do tell him, "I didn't say I was scared."

"You didn't have to."

Oh.

Okay, then.

THE BAKERY DOESN'T OPEN AT ALL ON FRIDAY.

By the time me and Gus made it back, it would've been pointless to even try. I had the kitchen to worry about, the ovens to clean, and the eerie sense that Declan Rowe's ghost was haunting the back alley. I didn't look. I couldn't bring myself to, and I was just glad that Gus pointedly avoided the door as much as I did.

Stuffed full of fruit, he curled up and napped on my side of the counter while I locked up behind me, then disappeared into the kitchen. About a half an hour into my clean, he threw his weight against the swinging door, waddling into the kitchen so he could keep me company during my attempt to tidy up my latest mess.

Even counting all the usual prep for the morning, we were heading upstairs about an hour before the bakery's usual closing time. Considering the day we'd had, both Gus and I agreed that we deserved an early night in.

Suddenly, it was five o'clock in the morning, Saturday, and I was determined to return to work. It was a fluke. That's what I told myself. Something terrible happened to that predator, but an even fiercer predator was on the case. I was just in the wrong spot at the wrong time. The sheriff had to know that.

He *had* to.

So I did what I always do, baking a little extra—and nothing charmed today, thank you very much—for the customers who missed out on yesterday. By the time eight o'clock rolled around I was ready to open.

Open, maybe, but deal with a scowling Roxy who pushed open the door the second after I unlocked it?

Yeah. That was a little more of a challenge.

She whirls on me. Her hair is loose, drawing attention to the largest white streak that travels from her part all the way down the length of her hair on the right side. She has on a black t-shirt that says 'wild thing' sprawled across her chest and the deep circles under her eyes are more purple than usual.

Her hands go right to her hips. "Honey. Shit. When I said something about dead bodies, I was just fucking around."

I wince. "You heard?"

"All of Moonburrow's heard!"

Damn. I was hoping that wasn't the case.

I don't know what I expected. Gossip travels fast in a small town. Throw in the fact that Declan was a member of the Moonshadow Pack and it would've passed down to the lowest-ranked shifters in no time. As a prey shifter and the sole proprietor of a junk/oddities shop—seriously, that's what Roxy called herself when I asked what she was doing these days—she doesn't stick her snout in pack politics, though she eventually digs out the details.

She must've been waiting for me to open to fill her in on my side of what happened. I don't know if I should be touched or annoyed when she snags a brownie from my sample try, grabs one of the empty seats at an empty table, drops into it backward, and looks at me expectantly.

Knowing better than to shut Roxy down, I tell her as much as I can. She snorts when I mention that Sheriff Lobo and his right-hand wolf are treating me like a suspect, and gets a thoughtful expression when she muses about who would want Declan Rowe dead.

"You've been living here a while," I say.

"Yup. About four years. I couldn't take living with my sister anymore back home so I searched for a nearby supe town and found Moonburrow."

Roxy's older sister Crystal is... well, a frenemy still means you can be friendly. Crystal only has enemies, and even when Roxy was the only one in her corner, my impression was that Crystal treated her worst of all.

Pointing that out might add the -enemy back to what kind of weird relationship we have going these days. Instead, I ask, "What do you think? You know the town much better. Any suspects?"

She raises her eyebrows. "Careful, Honey. If I didn't know better, I'd think you were going to play Miss Marple. You into mystery solving?"

"I'm into clearing my name."

"Well, if I hear any whispers, I'll let you know." She glances around as though she just noticed that we were missing an opossum-shaped lump. "Hey. Where's the rat— sorry. Gus. He okay?"

I try to hide the smile tugging at my lips. It took her a minute, but it's nice to see she cares. "I thought it might be a good idea to let him rest upstairs."

I thought it would be. Gus... he had a different opinion. He pouted when I said he could have the whole upstairs apartment—and my bed—to himself, but since I didn't know what to expect today, I wanted to keep him safe.

Am I being ridiculous? Maybe. I don't care, and if Roxy teases me about Gus, I'll move the brownies out of her reach so that she can't take another one.

Surprisingly, she doesn't have a snarky retort. In fact, she cocks her head, listening for something. I'm confused... but only until the whisper of pine ticking my nostrils becomes stronger and stronger an instant before the door opens, revealing—

"Sheriff Lobo!"

Because it's Sheriff Lobo.

He's wearing a tight dark blue t-shirt and jeans a shade lighter. His badge is hanging on his hip like usual, and he has a delicious amount of stubble on his jaw. Walking into the bakery, he frowns for a moment, shakes his head, and stalks right toward me.

Roxy's whole countenance changes. She rises up from the seat, her earlier interest and concern transforming to a seductive tease as she locks her gaze on the wolf.

What the...

"Look who's here. I didn't expect a wolf prowling around so early. You, Hon? C'mon out. Let's greet the sheriff."

What is she doing? Oh. I know.

Fucking with me.

"Roxy—"

She sidles up next to him. "Stop me if you heard this before. A wolf, a raccoon, and an opossum walk into a bakery..."

Let me just say that, if I hadn't already confessed my shifter side to the sheriff yesterday, I'd be super pissed at her for blowing up my spot like that. So maybe she didn't know it was a secret. Still. What is she doing *now*?

Her yellow eyes flash hypnotically, her attention completely on Sheriff Lobo. "Hey, handsome. Did

Honey tell you that opossums have an odd number of nipples?"

Oh. My. *God.*

I'm going to kill her. Sure, she's a raccoon, but she's not a big cat or a wolf. I can take her.

"That's wild opossums, Roxy," I say through gritted teeth. "Opossum shifters have the normal amount." I glance at the sheriff. He has a strange look on his face, and I'm not sure if it's the way that Roxy blatantly hit on him or, you know, the whole 'opossums having thirteen long, spaghetti-like nipples in the wild' thing. It's probably both. "Two," I blurt out. For some reason— and I'm not examining it too closely while pretending he isn't my mate—it seems important that he doesn't think I'm any weirder than I already am. "I have two."

He nods solemnly.

Roxy snickers.

My teeth are sharp. If I go for the carotid—

No. We're friends now. Kind of. Besides, while her tone is teasing, the fierce look in her deep yellow eyes is still locked on the sheriff. Alpha or not, there's a warning in her glare as she shifts her position, putting her long, lean body in between the wolf and me.

"That's right. And you're a specific type of opossum, ain'tcha, Hon? What was it again?"

"A Virgin—"

She winces, and I want to slap myself upside the head for setting her up so perfectly as she says, "Still?

Aren't you, like, pushing thirty? Shouldn't you have a mate by now?"

Little pieces. *Tiny* pieces. Scattered in as many dumpsters as I can find so that my currently least favorite trash panda can find eternal rest in *her* favorite place. "A Virginia opossum." My cheeks heat up. "And my mating is my business. What about you? Where's yours?"

She flashes her fangs at me, and I swear it's the first honest grin she's worn since the sheriff walked in the door. "My prince charming is going to work for me. When I'm ready, I'll find him. Right, Max?"

Max.

She gets to call him *Max*?

I glance at Sheriff Lobo, taking a step back when I notice that he's watching me. Not Roxy. During the whole strange exchange, he's been looking at *me*.

I cross my arms over my chest. "Yes?"

The sheriff gives me another look, even stranger this time. Stranger, and a whole lot more calculating. "You don't have a mate?"

Danger. Danger.

Shit.

CHAPTER 7
ROXY AND MAX

Where did *that* come from? Because while Roxy might've picked up on something twanging between me and the wolf, I have my scent-dampener potion on. He won't be able to recognize me... right?

I can't lie, either. I *won't* lie. Improving the truth... keeping it from him... faking it... that's one thing. But flat-out lying to my fated mate? My inner opossum won't let me even if I didn't have to worry about an Alpha being a truth detector.

I shake my head. "Not yet."

Emphasis on the *yet*.

"But what about—" He shakes his head. "Never mind. I'm here to—"

Hang on. "You thought the opossum I brought with me to the station was a shifter."

Sheriff Lobo has the good grace to look embarrassed. "It's a logical conclusion. If I was walking around Moonburrow with a wolf, you'd think he was one of mine."

"Yeah, because loose wolves don't go for a stroll down Sycamore Street. Gus is a wild opossum that I rescued as a young pup." My eyes widen. "You thought I mated him."

His expression turns defensive. "You're an opossum... he's an opossum..."

Ugh. "What are you, a speciesist?" My hands drop to my hips. For a moment, I completely forget that we have an audience. "What's next, Sheriff? Prey and predators shouldn't mix?"

"Ms. Morgan... Honey. I am all in support of mixed matings. I don't have a mate, either. But if she were human, prey, witch... I would accept her no matter what. When I find her, that is. I'm not here to discuss that, though. I'm here about Declan's murder."

Oh. Well. His softly stated comment really takes the wind out of my sails because, whether he knows it or not, he went from triggering my worst fear—that a wolf Alpha would never be happy with a prey shifter—to confirming that he would be... if she were his fated mate. I am, but he's right. This isn't the time to talk about that.

Murder trumps mating, simple as that.

Still, something changes in that moment. I notice it. The way Roxy suddenly backs off, her wild energy dimming as she slinks away from the sheriff and me, she notices it, too.

Since Declan's unfortunate murder, I've been a suspect. The spark in his gold wolf eyes suddenly says: *female.*

As long as it's not *mate* yet.

Roxy doesn't know that I recognized him as my mate months ago. No one knows. I'd bet that Roxy was just trying to break the ice, break the tension by being her obnoxious self. Or maybe she's trying to keep us all distracted for the moment for her own reasons until the air becomes charged with a different type of tension because, suddenly, she's behind the counter.

"On that note..." Roxy reaches into the pastry display, snagging a pumpkin spice muffin in each hand. She shows them off. "Gotta love dexterous fingers. Score one for us prey shifters."

Sheriff Lobo scowls. "Don't you think it's a bad idea to commit petty theft right in front of Moonburrow's sheriff? Because I'm right here, Roxy, and I don't see you reaching for some money to pay for those. I could arrest you, you know."

"You tell yourself that, handsome. Honey? We'll chat later. 'Kay. Ciao."

And, taking a careful bite from the muffin while stalking around the counter, cutting specifically through the few feet of space separating me and the sheriff, she waggles her fingers and disappears out the front door of the bakery.

There are no other customers inside. Just me. Just Sheriff Lobo.

Damn. Maybe I shouldn't have left Gus upstairs.

I could've used the moral support.

"So... I guess you've met Roxy Kane?"

Crap. I was just about to ask him the same question. In my head, both the sheriff and my old frenemy existed in Moonburrow. Interacting, though? Nah. They were totally separate. Moonburrow has about a thousand occupants. It's a small supernatural town, but not so small that I expected the sheriff to know *every* member of his pack.

Then again, this is *Roxy*. With her personality and belief that laws exist for shifters who don't have white streaks running through their hair, I'm not surprised that she's acquainted with Sheriff Lobo.

I'm not surprised. Jealous, though? That's a totally different story.

And speaking of stories...

"We go way back. One time, when we were in high school, she was missing during the period before lunch. No one could find her. Eventually, her sister mentioned that Roxy had said she might be peckish. We eventually found her snoring in a dumpster. The lid had shut while she was going through the trash for a snack, and when she couldn't get out again, she said screw it and took a nap."

I remember how everyone started mockingly calling her a trash panda after that. She leaned into it, styling her hair so that the white streaks were more prominent. Then there were the purple circles under her yellow eyes that marked her as a raccoon. As though she was sticking her middle finger up at the rest of the school, she started to color them in with black eyeliner.

It was like she was saying, you think I'm a raccoon all the time, I'll be a raccoon. She didn't care what anyone thought, and a part of me envied that. It wasn't until much later that I realized that Crystal had known where she would be because *Crystal* had been the one to shut the lid on Roxy while she was dumpster-diving, and I almost admired her more for glaring at the world after it tried to make her a victim.

Of course, almost immediately, she 'accidentally' got a wad of pink bubblegum in my hair, positioned in such a spot that I had to hack off eight inches. After it finally grew out, I got into the habit of doing a loose braid on both sides of my head, resting the hair over my shoulder. That way, if it happened again, maybe I could only lose a lock instead of most of the back.

Twelve years later, I still wear my hair the same way, and I have Roxy Kane to thank for it.

"High school?" echoes the sheriff, as though he's having a hard time believing that could be true. "You've known her that long?"

"Longer," I admit. "We were technically in the same pack when we both lived in this small shifter town in Virginia. I grew up with her."

"You're friends?"

"Sometimes."

He quirks an eyebrow at me.

What can I say? *Sometimes* is a pretty accurate description of our relationship these days.

Sure, she teased me when we were younger. When I got my first crush on a porcupine shifter, she made sure to tell him—then later went with him to the end of school dance. She also got into a very fierce catfight with a, well, cat when a stray chased me home during an unexpected shift. I ended up falling over, playing dead in my actual opossum shape, and if Roxy hadn't intercepted the hungry tom, that might've been it for me. Instead, she shifted to her raccoon, beat the shit out of the cat until it ran off our turf, then moaned about how I owed her twenty bucks because the shift ruined her favorite vintage tee.

We have a past, and though Roxy Kane was the last person I expected to see in Moonburrow, a couple of pilfered pastries now and then is a fair price to pay to feel like someone has my back.

Even if I might claw out her yellow eyes if I really thought she was hitting on Max instead of doing the Roxy special of just making everyone around us uncomfortable...

"She doesn't respect me as her Alpha." He frowns. "She doesn't seem to respect you as her friend, either."

I snort. "Roxy doesn't respect anyone except Roxy."

He tilts his head, a silent agreement to my very astute observation.

Oof. It's such a simple gesture, but the way it shows off the thick column of his throat, the length of his eyelashes, and the power in his shoulders... uh-oh. I'm in trouble. Without Roxy to act as a buffer, I'm getting the full blast of the sheriff—and my inner opossum is perking up, begging for his attention.

Down, girl. He's the *sheriff*. Right now, after what happened yesterday, I don't think I want his attention... not if that's all he can be to me.

Sheriff, I tell myself. He's the sheriff—

"So what brings you by?" I ask. Okay. It comes out more like a squeak, but the sooner I understand the reason why he's here, the sooner I can wave him out my door.

He gives his head a small clearing shake, like he forgot there was more to his visit than threatening to arrest Roxy.

"Right. Yes. I came over in person because I wanted to tell you that one of my team tested the cupcake. You were right. No magic."

So he did get it tested? Phew. I knew it would help me prove my innocence.

"Oh, thank goodn—"

"No magic," he echoes. "Just straight shifter poison."

I'm sorry. *What*?

Whoops. There I go. My knees wobble. My body locks. I'm just about to drop—

"Easy, killer." He grabs my arm, steadying me. "I got you."

The dark spots on the edge of my vision vanish in an instant the moment his warm paw lands on my upper arm, nearly searing me through my shirt.

"You okay?"

Shockingly, I *am*. "Yeah. I think so. But... I didn't do it. Whatever was in that cupcake, I didn't put it there."

He releases me. I bite back a sound of utter disappointment as he rumbles, "I know."

Wait—

He does?

"You... *do*?" Relief rushes through me. I want to throw my arms around him, but that just might be my inner opossum talking, wanting a little more skin-to-skin contact with her mate. "Sheriff Lobo—"

"Max."

I startle. "What?"

Hands returning to the back pockets of his jeans, he shrugs. "You gave me permission to call you by your name. You're one of mine now. I'm not just the sheriff. I'm your Alpha. I'm Max."

If he actually means what he says, I *should* be calling him 'Alpha'. It's the proper way to address the leader of the pack, though not even Colin pushed us to use the term unless it was important. Opossums are almost as ungovernable as raccoons, mainly because we either hiss or drop. There is no in-between.

Only I didn't drop. I thought I was seconds away from fainting, and then Sheriff Lobo—no, Max... he's *Max*—hurriedly reached out, steadying my arm, and the light-headedness that precedes an entire Honey shutdown simply went away.

Oh, that can't be good.

I glance up at him. There's that curious look on his

face again. Like he's searching for something, but even he doesn't know what it is.

"One of our packmates"—our packmates, he's calling them *our* packmates—"is a chemist. They called in some favors and we were able to figure out that the poison was sprinkled on top of the cupcake. It glittered—"

"The cupcake I made for you didn't glitter," I tell him. "I put crushed caramel candies on top of the frosting as a garnish. That was it."

"Right. The glitter was only obvious under a microscope. It was silver, Honey. He ingested straight silver cut with wolfsbane and something they haven't figured out yet, but it's deadly to supes. You're a supe. Unless you're a sadistic possum, I'm pretty sure someone else laced my cupcake."

I blink. A heartbeat later, I start to sway.

His cupcake. That's right. If Declan gave it to him after it was poisoned, Max could've died. He could've died and I would never have had the chance to confess that he's my mate...

Max wraps his arm around my back, keeping me on my feet. "Oh no you don't. You're not in danger, Honey. No need for any of that."

I want to believe that. Not in danger... someone used one of my cupcakes as a vessel to commit wolficide. Maybe I'm not in danger, but what about him?

"Could it have been Declan?" I ask. "He's the only

one I gave that cupcake to. I didn't even make a batch. It was special."

My ears burn at the tops. Oh, boy. Now you've done it, Honey. You just admitted to Max that it was more than a simple peace offering—

"We don't know. He was a good wolf, a decent delta, and he did a great job managing the only gym we have in Moonburrow. I don't know why he had my cupcake, why he didn't give it to me at the pack meet, or how he ended up being poisoned by it, but I just wanted to assure you that I *will* find out. That's my job."

Of course it is. He's the Alpha *and* the sheriff. He'll solve the crime.

And whether he wants me to or not, I'll help.

———

THAT, OF COURSE, IS EASIER SAID THAN DONE.

I'm no Miss Marple. I'm no Jessica Fletcher. I'm none of those old lady amateur sleuths that I only know about because I spent a lot of my youth at Grandma Jean and Grandpa Gary's house. I have no idea how to even start investigating what happened to Declan, and I spend the rest of the morning after Max left the bakery trying to come up with something that might resemble a lead.

Murder mysteries make it seem so easy. You have a victim. You have a cause of death. I think about what

Max said. According to his chemist, the poison was made up of three things: silver, wolfsbane, and a secret third thing.

Shoot. It doesn't even need to have a third thing at all. Silver is a huge threat to shifters. It burns our skin; I can't even imagine the danger it would do if ingested. Wolfsbane—or aconite—is a plant that nukes so many of our abilities. It was initially farmed to ward off 'werewolves', but that's because it works. Wolfsbane doesn't just repel shifters. It does something to our senses. When wolfsbane is involved, we don't hear as well, scent as well, or heal as well.

The only other element that messes with shifters that I know of is mercury. Add a little of that to any poison and you can do nasty damage. I heard a story about someone who had their soda spiked with it. While mercury isn't as powerful as wolfsbane or silver, it's insidious in how it cuts us off from our inner beast until it wears off.

It wouldn't make a good poison. Oh, no. That's the silver and the wolfsbane, and since I don't have a clue what to do with that information, I just tuck it in a corner of my brain so that I can focus on helping my customers.

News spread even further. Of course it did. I've seen twice as many customers at this point today than I ever had, and it doesn't take an amazing detective to figure out it's because my bakery is the scene of a crime. It doesn't matter if Declan's body was found out back. It was on my territory, with one of my cupcakes. Shifters can be a morbid bunch sometimes. I wouldn't be surprised that my customers were clearing me out of my stock in case I suddenly decided to go straight murderess. Like they wanted to see if I served them a poisoned cupcake, would they survive?

Hey. It's money in the register, and if they want to roll the dice, maybe I should whip up another batch of Can't Resist Cupcakes. At least then they'd get something tasty, and maybe I could get some answers.

I don't, but that's because I promised Sheriff Lobo —*Max*—that I wouldn't bake them for any paying customers in Moonburrow again. However, it does give me an idea.

People gossip in Moonburrow. I usually drown it out, busy as I am, but today... today I listen.

And I strike gold.

A little before I was getting ready to close for the day, a wolf shifter female and a jaguar male come into the bakery together. I don't remember seeing them before, but as they're both predators, I figure they might be higher up in the Moonshadow Pack than someone like me or Roxy or Fannie the fox shifter.

Maybe they are. Or maybe they just thought they were better than me and I only existed to ring them up some cranberry and orange scones because they walked in while in the middle of a conversation and only paused it to place their order.

They were rude, but they were very helpful. Just as the wolf shifter was handing over her card to pay, she said, "Wolfsbane. Yeah."

My ears perk up. *Wolfsbane, you say...*

The jaguar frowned. "I thought the Alpha refused to let anyone have wolfsbane in Moonburrow."

Makes sense. If I was the Alpha, I'd bar that from a supe town, too. Sure, it has some beneficial properties—mainly for witches and their potions, like my scent-dampening charm—but the risks don't outweigh those benefits.

"Of course he does," cuts in the wolf. "Only the apothecary carries it. Good thing Joey's got a part-time job over there, working for the witch who runs it. It's the only place you can get your paws on the stuff in town."

"And it doesn't bother him?"

The wolf female shrugs. "He's a rat. Nothing bothers him." Her head turns, gold eyes looking me over as I do my best to appear innocent. *No, I'm not eavesdropping on every word you say, why do you ask?* She taps her nails on the top of the pastry display, the tips of her claws clicking against the glass. "My card? Our scones?"

Oh. Right. I hand her the debit card still in my hand, then pass her the bag full of scones she ordered.

She flashes me a smile that's all fang before bumping her hip into that of her companion. Nodding at the door, she heads for it without so much as a 'thank you'.

That's okay. I should be thanking her for my first lead.

As soon as I close, it looks like I'm going to see a rat about some wolfsbane.

CHAPTER 8
PREY CIRCLE

Welp. That was the plan, at least.

I had every intention of finishing up my closing duties, feeding Gus dinner, grabbing something quick to eat myself, then taking a trip across Moonburrow. Right after those two customers left, I checked to make sure no one else had entered Dough You Believe in Magic before reaching for my phone.

I try not to keep it out when I'm working. I'm a one-female show here. I joke that Gus manages the bakery, but it's pretty much the truth. He supervises; I do everything else. I'm already so busy. If I distract myself with my phone, I'll never get it done.

Of course, that means that my family knows that they can't reach me during the day. That doesn't stop Mom from trying, and when I saw she called me three times and checked in by text, I resigned myself to the inevitable.

I usually talk to my parents at least once a week. Anything more has me wanting to bash my head into the nearest flat surface. Anything less and Mom starts getting the idea that I'm avoiding them, that maybe it's time I give up on living by myself and return to Onancock.

Pass. I bet there are at least four opossum males she was ready to introduce me to as a prospective mate. She wants me to return to the clan, settle down, start a family. I told her jokingly once that I have. That Gus is my son. She wasn't amused.

Hm. I wonder how she would react if I mentioned that Max got the ridiculous idea that Gus is my *mate...*

We've come to a small compromise. I let them know that I'm alive and well, Mom and Dad don't hop in a car and drive from Virginia to Maryland. It's not that far of a drive, but I much prefer loving my parents from a distance. Even if that means that I get stuck on the phone with her for over an hour, doing mental gymnastics to keep from blurting out: *I found a dead predator who was killed with one of my cupcakes.*

Somehow, I manage, though I'll tell you that the evening chat got a whole lot longer when, suddenly, she put me on hold and, when she came back on the line, she had *Grandma Jean* with her.

You think an Alpha is an excellent lie detector? Max has nothing on a witch who mated an opossum shifter and watched her daughter do the same.

Of course, that just meant that I couldn't lie to Grandma Jean. That was easy. Everything I told her was the truth. About how successful the bakery has been since I took over, how I've met some of her old friends... I even reluctantly confessed to the Can't Resist Cupcakes fiasco.

Pro-tip from me to you. If you don't want to get in trouble for a big thing—like, I don't know, getting yourself involved in a murder mystery—then you should take the knock and admit to something less worrisome. Mom was horrified, but Grandma Jean just laughed in that husky way she has, warning me to read all the fine print when it comes to the recipes in her book.

She did offer to cut her trip to Europe short. If Moonburrow needed her... if *I* needed her... she'd come back tomorrow.

When I jumped in and hurriedly assured them both that I was fine and that Grandma Jean shouldn't have to change her plans for my sake, my words rang with absolute truth. I'm already in this mess. I don't need to get my family caught up in it, too.

By the end, Mom agreed to stay in Virginia, Grandma was getting ready to visit Spain, and I had to swallow my disappointment that it was probably too late to go to the apothecary.

I looked it up earlier. I didn't even know Moonburrow had an apothecary, but considering there were more than a few witches who made up their small coven in town, I guess it made sense. Witches 'n' Things was about a ten-minute ride to the east end of Moonburrow, in a decidedly more… witchy side of town. There was a coffee shop with skulls in the window on one side of it; a hattery with a tendency to the more pointed kinds on the other.

Saturday was out. However, after another busy day at the bakery, I decided to take the drive over after we closed Sunday night. The day was full of customers, but not leads. Roxy was MIA, and I didn't hear anything from Max. A few customers were still eyeballing the bakery as though they expected I had a murderer behind my counter, only to be slightly disappointed when all I was harboring was an opossum who was crunching noisily on a dish of peanuts I set aside for him.

After closing, I pocketed my phone without looking at it. I didn't even stop for dinner, and with a belly full of peanuts, Gus didn't hiss in annoyance when I told him we were going to the car.

Gus is the perfect passenger princess. He likes to curl up on the passenger seat, chirping at me until I engage the seat warmer. I just plugged in the address and hoped for the best.

It's five-thirty in the evening on a Sunday. You'd think there would be street parking, but Luck is still having her fun, messing with me. I ended up having to find a parking lot about four blocks away before I could find a spot. I patted my shoulder, Gus climbed into his customary spot, and away we went.

The smell of hundreds of different powerful herbs warring with each other perfume the street. I know we're approaching before we even arrive, it's that strong. It hits me that this shop is probably where Grandma Jean gets most of the supplies for her charmed cupcakes. Who knows, maybe if this lead washes out, at least I'll know where to refill her herbs and powders whenever I start to run low.

It's an idea, and it might even have been a good one —if the store wasn't dark, the door locked, and the sign on the window saying:

Store hours: when the moon is high or the tide is full or the songbirds sing

Huh?

It's closed. Obviously. But with hours like that, I have no idea how I'm ever going to have a chance to talk to this Joey.

I grab the door, giving it another frustrated tug.

"It's best if you book an appointment," comes a soft, gentle female voice.

I turn around quickly.

Someone had snuck up right behind me. And maybe I should be more on my toes if we have a murderer in Moonburrow, but one look at her, and I quickly dismiss her as a prospective suspect.

Seeing me look at her, she flinches, then straightens. It's an instinctive response for some prey shifters. Opossums play dead when they feel like they're in danger. Raccoons cause chaos. Bunnies hop away, and deer stand frozen for a second before deciding whether they should flee or hold their ground.

Everything about this female tells me that she's a doe. From her wide dark eyes to her dusky skin and short bobbed haircut streaked with amber and brown, she's delicate, yet willowy, and she's wearing an apologetic expression at odds with her basic black business dress.

She can recognize that I'm no predator. I'm probably one of the least dominant shifters in Moonburrow so she has nothing to be afraid of. Add my opossum accessory, and she seems more at ease as the seconds pass.

"I'm sorry. Did you say something about an appointment?"

She nods. "I have my office right next door. The witch who owns it is… she's a unique spirit. She opens the store when she's in the mood, but if you go online and book an appointment, she almost always will be in." She pauses for a moment, nose wrinkling a bit as she says helpfully, "She has an app!"

Right. A witch with an app. Of course.

But how do I get in touch with Joey the rat?

"Oh. Thanks. But I was actually hoping to see my good friend Joey. I haven't been able to get in touch with him lately."

If she knows I'm full of shit, she has the decency not to call me out on it. "In that case, come to the prey circle meeting tomorrow night! I always go. Joey never misses a meeting. You're a prey shifter, right?"

I nod, not bothering to hide that fact much longer. At this rate, with the gossips working over time, my opossum side will be common knowledge.

Fun times. If my new neighbors are anything like Roxy and her crew used to be, I can depend on some of them trying to scare me to see if I really *do* play possum…

Hopefully she's not one of them if her enthusiasm is anything to go by. "Great. You should come!"

I never thought I'd go to a prey circle meeting

when Betsy mentioned it to me the other day. Then I said: *never say never.* Looks like I was right.

"So... what time does the meeting start?"

THE MOONBURROW COMMUNITY CENTER SMELLS faintly of sawdust, lemon cleaner, and nervous sweat. It's the unofficial perfume of prey shifters, and it irks me how much it reminds me of home.

It's a handful of minutes before seven o'clock. The meeting starts promptly at seven, but I didn't want to seem too eager—or give me the chance to wimp out—so I'm only just walking in now.

No Gus. I'll have to make it up to him, but he's a wild opossum. While he'll hiss and play dead when frightened, he has his size against him. Wild opossums have been known to capture and eat rats. I don't want to make Joey nervous. If he comes to the prey circle meetings, he's probably the nervous sort, and it's easy to look at me with my blonde hair and purple eyes and think I won't try to eat his beast. But Gus... it's better to keep him safe back at the bakery.

Not saying my little sidekick is *happy* about that, but since I gave him a roll, some oats, a sliced apple, and let him sleep in the basket downstairs so he could watch over the bakery while I was gone, he'll be fine.

Here's hoping I will be, too.

The folding chairs in the otherwise empty room are arranged in a half-circle beneath bright fluorescent lights. A handwritten sign is taped to the open door. It says:

PREY CIRCLE:
Safe, Supportive, and Non-Predatory

Below that, in much smaller handwriting: *Snacks provided. No sudden movements, please.*

I take a seat near the end, clutching my purse like a life raft. Gus would've loved this—all the twitchy energy, the snacks, the *gossip* already passing through the others—but when I pick out one male out of the group of seven prey shifters, I'm grateful I left him behind.

Not all shifters look like their wild counterparts. The doe shifter I met—who is sitting opposite of me—definitely does. So does Frannie. Betsy has pink eyes, and Roxy has purple circles. Joey... he twitches. Assuming he's the rat I want to talk to, he looks like a regular, ordinary human male in his early twenties. Light brown hair. Dark brown eyes. A slight build... but, oh, the twitching.

Yup. He's nervous alright.

I wonder why?

The meeting starts when Betsy bounces up first, standing in the center of the half-circle. "Welcome, everyone! I'm so glad you came to tonight's prey circle. Since we have a new member joining us tonight, why don't we start with names and one thing that's been on our minds this week."

She points at the plump female with dark skin and even darker eyes sitting next to me. I guess, as the newbie, I'll go last.

My neighbor squeaks. Mouse, I think. Joey is a rat, but this female has got to be a mouse.

"Hi. I'm Marnie. And I'm just grateful no hawks have moved into Moonburrow this month."

Yup. I was right. Total mouse.

Polite laughter follows. It's that high, strained kind that means we all know it's not entirely a joke.

Up next is a tall, striking female with black hair and white stripes like Roxy—only she's not a raccoon. She's a skunk, and the reason why there's the distinct stink of sawdust in the air. It's an ingredient in the scent-dampener charm. No wonder I'm relying on physical characteristics to guess what my fellow prey shifters are. Apart from picking up on the lemon freshener and sweat, their individual scents are muted.

Phew. That means mine is, too.

Her name is Caroline, and she's been thinking about telling her wolf neighbor that his nightly howling at the moon is getting obnoxious. The other prey shifters commiserate, but no one has any advice for her.

If we can help it, we don't go up against predators. Unless, of course, we have the unbreakable protection of one...

Betsy goes next, then it's Joey's turn.

I lean forward in my seat.

"Joey," he says, and I swallow my sound of relief that he *is* Joey. "And I got a new job this week. My old boss let me go two weeks ago because she didn't have the hours, but I was able to move from stocking shelves at the apothecary to delivering pizza for Carlo's. I work five days a week now."

Betsy nods approvingly. "That's great, Joey. Keeping busy helps the nerves."

Keeping busy does, but if he stopped working at the apothecary two weeks ago, what are the chances that he can give me any information about recent wolfsbane deliveries?

I hide my disappointment, hoping to get my features under control as the doe shifter I spoke to this afternoon lifts her slender hand.

"I'm Abigail. And... I think I'm dating a predator."

A hush falls over the room. Someone drops their carrot stick.

Betsy's voice turns careful. "You think?"

Abigail blushes, tucking a hunk of hair behind one long, elegant ear. "He's sweet, really. Keeps telling me he'd never hurt me. But he doesn't like it when I come here." Her voice falters, that same apologetic smile on her face that I saw earlier. "Says it makes me scared of him. I told him that's not it. I just like being around others like me."

Betsy gives her a sympathetic smile. "You're allowed to have a safe space. That's what this is."

It's Joey's turn to lean forward, concern wrinkling his forehead. "Is he your mate?"

"He says he might be. My doe thinks he could be. But she... she's skittish."

I know what that's like. The first time I caught Max's scent, I couldn't believe he could be my mate. Then I realized he was a predator, and I didn't think he *could* be. Now... I don't know what he is, but I can't let anyone hurt him.

Same with Abigail. I just met her, but she seems sweet. "Hey. If he ever scares you, I bake a mean Leave Me Alone Muffin. Anyone who eats it gets explosive diarrhea, giving you time to get away while smirking at the predator terrorizing you."

A ripple of laughter moves through the circle, lightening the mood. Even Joey grins.

"Honey is our new town baker." Betsy gestures at me. "Go on. Introduce yourself to the rest of us, sweetie."

Oh. Right.

"So, uh, I'm Honey Morgan. I bake."

And the only thing that's on my mind is that

murder that none of the prey shifters in this room have mentioned once...

Caroline's lips part. "I heard of you. Dough You Believe in Magic, right? You're the reason Frannie has to wear a wig until her fur grows back."

I wince. "Well, actually, that was the witch's fault—"

Caroline snickers. "Frannie deserved it. Charging a hundred dollars for a haircut while using box dye on her tail. I'm glad it came out." She pauses. "But if you ever use one of your charmed cupcakes on me like that, I'll spray you so hard, it'll never come out."

See? That right there is why not all prey shifters are defenseless. Roxy sure as hell isn't, and I wonder if she knows Caroline. Something tells me they would be great friends if they haven't already met.

Great friends, or the worst of enemies.

Once I assure them that that was an accident, and that I've put a hold on charmed cupcakes unless they've been specifically requested, the mood shifts.

The conversation drifts to harmless topics. Zoning permits, taxes, which grocery stores are the friendliest to all supes. I join in half-heartedly, the image of Abigail's nervous smile lingering in my mind as the meeting eventually ends.

> About time.
>
> — GUS

E ven if I wanted to take a few minutes to talk to Joey, that's impossible. The moment Betsy announces that the meeting is over, he high-tails it out the door, leaving the rest of us to fold the chairs and stack them against the wall.

That seems to be a common enough occurrence that not even Caroline complains about it. She just folds up Joey's chair and carries it over with hers. Betsy tells us all to take the leftover snacks home, then reminds the prey circle that the next meeting is in two weeks.

I... might come back. Who knows? I have Gus and I have Roxy, but maybe it won't be such a bad idea to make a few friends in Moonburrow. I think of Abigail again. She seems nice, and she might need a friend, too, in case her predator mate becomes a problem.

She hangs back for a few minutes, but when everyone's packing up, saying goodbye and heading out the door, she walks over to me. This smile is another shy one, and she's digging into her oversized tote as she approaches.

She pulls out a small pink mesh sachet with something in it. The scent-dampener charm in the room makes it hard for me to tell what it is, but she seems proud of it.

"For you," she says. "Comfort tea with chamomile. I make the blend myself. It helps with the nerves. I give some to everyone who comes to the prey circle meetings."

"Oh, that's so sweet—"

She touches my arm, a fleeting brushing of her fingers against my sleeve. "It works best at night. A little hot water, some milk if you like. It's good for you."

I nod, promising I'll try, even though I know I probably won't. I'm not really a chamomile tea person. Still, if she's being friendly enough to offer me some of her special brew, I'll take it with me.

"It was nice to meet you, Honey."

I nod. "You, too. Be careful."

"Thank you. I will."

Tucking the sachet into my purse, I head out the door.

When I step outside, the night air feels heavier than before. The moon looks too bright, the shadows too long, and somewhere in the back of my mind, something small and instinctive whispers: *run*.

There's a predator lurking. For a moment, I freeze, then I force myself to take another few steps away from the community center and the scent-dampener charm inside of the main room. It wears off slowly, and by the time I see the tall figure separating himself from the shadows on the corner, I get a fresh whiff of pine.

Max.

"Honey? Is that you?"

Busted.

I adjust my hold on my purse, turning toward the sheriff. "Max. How are you? What are you doing here?"

"A lead I was following for my current case." Declan's murder. "He slipped away through another entrance, but I thought..." He gives his head a short shake. "You're here. Why are you here?"

Something tells me that, if I say I'm here for the same reason he is, he's not going to be happy. "I came by to check out the prey circle meeting. Betsy invited me the other day. I was bored. It seemed like it might be interesting."

And if you're here because you were looking for

Joey the rat—the 'he' kinda gives that away—then we really were both heading down the same path, looking for his murderer…

Max can tell. I don't know how. I don't know why. I didn't *lie* to him so it's not like he can scent any deception. Still… he *knows*.

He exhales through his nose, that tiny yet obvious sign of his wolf peeking through. If it was anyone else, I'd be seeing spots on the corner of my eyes. But it's not anyone else.

It's Max.

"You're not bored, Honey. You're curious. And curiosity gets people hurt."

"Well," I say sweetly, moving a few steps in the direction of Sycamore Street, "I've already died once or twice or a hundred times, you know. Perk of being an opossum shifter. I don't worry about it."

His jaw twitches. He clearly hates my attempt at a joke, though he doesn't say so. Rather than do that, he moves with me. "Well, where are you going now? You shouldn't walk home alone."

"I didn't drive," I admit. "Wasn't worth the gas for, like, eight blocks so I have no choice. Besides, I'll be fine."

"Of course you will."

I look up at him in surprise. Predators like Max rarely admit that a prey shifter can take care of themselves. "Thank you—"

"Because I'll walk with you."

Oh, you've got to be kidding me. A babysitter? He wants to be my babysitter?

"I don't think—"

He's already matching my pace, long strides eating up the sidewalk. "Humor me."

I sigh, but don't argue. Whatever. It's eight blocks. So long as he stays quiet and I can keep my inner opossum from taking over, shifting, and throwing herself at his feet, I can make it home with my pride—and my secret—intact.

It's not easy. The more time I spend with Max, the more I don't understand why I can't just tell him the truth. At this point, I know I'll have to. The time when I believed that this could never work between us... that's over and done with. I would never forgive myself if I didn't *try*... but despite how he seems to actually have a vested interest in seeing me survive that goes past me being a possible murder suspect, he treats me like someone to protect.

Someone to coddle.

I don't want to be coddled. I want to be loved, and while Fate gives you a mate that you can't help but adore eventually, Max still has no clue that he's mine and I'm his.

It's the scent-dampener. That *zing* that comes with recognizing your fated mate... he hasn't felt it yet because I'm still hiding myself from him. And I have to.

At least until Declan's murderer is found and Dough You Believe in Me—and, you know, *me*—is exonerated in the eyes of Moonburrow, I have to keep my distance.

That's easier said than done considering he's inches away and all I want to do is throw myself into his arms.

He swings his. I didn't notice it before. When I think of Max, I think of stoic. Kind of grumpy. Determined to be in control. For some reason, that just translated to being stiff and still, but I'm so wrong. He prowls, stalks, moving with such a deceptively lazy grace, I can't help but be aware of his every movement.

There are accidental touches. Every time his hand brushes mine, my pulse jumps. My temperature rises. My breath catches. If he notices, he doesn't say, but how can he not notice?

What is going on here?

By the time we finally reach the bakery, the air between us feels too warm for mid-autumn. I'm almost burning up with things I can't say to Max, and he's just as quiet. Giving myself something to do, I grab my keys from my purse. I unlock the door and glance behind me. He's still there, broad and silent, and if I didn't know any better, I'd think he was a wolf trying to decide if he was on guard patrol or a *date*.

That seals it for me.

"Want to come in?" I ask, surprising both of us.

His brows lift. "You sure?"

Not even a little. "Yeah. You can check the place for monsters if it makes you feel better."

I'm teasing.

The door closes behind him with a soft click. The bakery smells like sugar and cinnamon, opossum—*Gus*—and a hint of pine that drives me wild.

He surveys the front room, doing his duty, then turns to me. "You need to be careful, Honey."

"I *am* careful."

"There's danger in Moonburrow."

I figured. "Right. Aren't the big, bad wolves supposed to keep me safe?"

That earns me a look: half exasperation, half something else. Something that makes my heart beat in triple-time.

His mouth quirks, a begrudging grin. "You're not scared of much, are you?"

"I'm scared of plenty," I say lightly. "I just hide it better than most prey. Unless I lose control and play dead, that is."

He steps closer. "Killer—"

I blink. "You've called me that before. You said you believed me when I told you I didn't have anything to do with Declan's death. So why are you teasing me like that?"

He hesitates, eyes searching mine. "You really want to know?"

"Yes."

He refuses to break eye contact with me. When it comes to the Alpha, this will be a challenge I have to win or lose—and as he makes a softly uttered confession that has me glancing away, I don't think either of us won.

"Because I don't want to see you dead. Calling you 'killer' feels better than thinking of you as another victim. I've been sheriff in Moonburrow for four years. Since I was twenty-seven and I took over the pack when my dad stepped down as Alpha. I got the badge and the top spot over Moonshadow... in all that time, the only deaths I've seen have been pack business. This one? It belongs to the sheriff. It's not the same even though you'd think it would be considering we lost one of our own."

The words knock the air right out of me. My throat tightens. "It's not just a case to you. As the Alpha... you had to handle a death of a packmate, too."

He nods once, jaw set. "Pack burial was this morning. I talked to Declan's mother. She asked me if he suffered. I didn't have an answer she'd want to hear." A soft snort. "Ripping out throats is easy to explain. But poison? Who poisons shifters? And why stop at one?"

His voice tells me he's sure there will be more deaths. The way he's watching me is a big clue that he thinks it might be me—but he doesn't want it to be.

I swallow hard, the sharp ache of sympathy and

something warmer catching me off guard. "You'll find who did this."

"I have to."

"I'll help," I say, softer than I mean to.

His eyes narrow, not in warning this time, but in open disbelief. "You're serious."

I don't understand why he seems so surprised. At the community center, he made it seem like he suspected I was doing some sleuthing on the side. Of course I want to help him. I shrug. "Yeah. I'm serious."

Suddenly, the air in the bakery changes. It's quiet, but it grows thicker. I nearly choke on the weight of the expectant look that fills his predatory gaze. His eyes... they're on me, roving over my face, taking in every detail of the opossum shifter daring to look back at the wolf.

There's something in that expression of his. Max looks down at me like he's not sure what he's seeing anymore: a nuisance or a helping hand. I'm not challenging him with eye contact; not like if I was anyone but *me*. I'm just there, and *there* is exactly where Max wants me.

His hand drops down, landing on my hip. I didn't even realize how close we were until I feel the heat of his paw through my shirt. He tugs on me, pulling me closer. At the same time, he bends his head slowly, so slow, I could duck out of his path. I could refuse him. I could get away.

I don't.

His other hand finds my jaw, rough thumb brushing the corner of my mouth. "You drive me insane, killer," he mutters.

"Good," I whisper back, breath coming quickly. I'll regret this in the morning. I know I will. But if I even try to escape my mate, my opossum will kill me. "Means we're even, Max."

He groans to hear me say his name. Maybe if I hadn't... maybe if I'd called him 'Sheriff' or 'Alpha', reminding him who he is... maybe then I could've stopped this. Only I didn't *want* to stop this.

I wanted him to kiss me—and that's exactly what Max does.

The second his mouth leaves mine, I'm glitching. Like my brain just short-circuited, which makes total sense. The potion might keep Max from realizing I'm his fated mate, but I've known who he was since the day I crossed into Moonburrow. This is all my opossum wanted, some sign that our mate might possibly choose us. For a second, I think I got it, and then I dare another peek up at his face.

His expression is so tortured, my stomach drops all the way to my shoes.

No.

No.

He didn't want his. Or he did, but he realizes it was a mistake.

I'm a mistake.

Ignoring my opossum's screech of heartache and pain, I duck out of his loose hold.

Max takes one step back, then another, until there's enough space between us that the temptation vanishes.

The temptation vanishes.

The tension lingers.

"Right," he says. His voice is lower, rougher. "That shouldn't have happened."

Fuck. That look on his face... I'd expected rejection. Doesn't mean it doesn't hurt.

I nod so hard I nearly pull my neck. "Of course. It was an accident. Totally random lipsmacking. Happens all the time in bakeries."

One dark brow lifts. "Does it now?"

"Constant hazard. Occupational risk. And I didn't even charm you."

The way his brow furrows says: didn't you?

He exhales through his nose, somewhere between a laugh and a growl, then rubs the back of his neck. "We forget it, then."

"Perfect. Forgotten. Never happened." I back toward the counter, desperate to put it between us. "You're still the sheriff, I'm still the—uh—mildly suspected baker."

And not his mate. How can I tell him I'm his fated mate in the middle of this mess? Especially since, if he still doesn't know, he's not looking too closely at me like a female. Not like he did that fleeting moment after Roxy mentioned I'm a Virginia opossum.

Oh, no. I was just the prey shifter who possibly poisoned one of his packmates… but if that's so, why did he kiss me?

My eyes are on his lips. As if he can sense them, his mouth twitches, the ghost of a smile he doesn't want me to see… but that he doesn't hide from regardless. "And you're still terrible at staying out of trouble."

I shrug. "What can I say? It's a consistent character trait."

He turns for the door, shaking his head slightly as he goes. "Lock up after me, Killer."

The surprisingly snarky nickname hits differently this time—less gruff, more like he's rolling it over in his mouth, tasting it, deciding it's more a tease than an accusation… but how is that possible when he still thinks I might have something to do with his packmate's death?

After Max is gone, I lean against the front counter, heart just about ready to beat its way out of my chest.

"Forget it," I whisper to myself. "Yep. Forgotten."

Gus chitters from his corner perch, calling me a liar.

"Don't start," I tell him. "It's not like the big, bad wolf just kissed me in my own bakery or anything."

He squeaks once—definitely laughter, the traitor—

and curls back on his self-proclaimed bag of flour throne.

Me? I run my trembling finger over my lip, trying to figure out how exactly I'm going to forget it when tasting Max Lobo was like coming home for the first time.

CHAPTER 10

PEPPERMINT AND POISON

Another not-possum playing dead, only she's not playing.

Mother is still not the murderer. I double-checked.

— GUS

There's nothing like a second murder to really ruin your week.

I wanted so desperately to believe that what happened to Declan Rowe was a one-off. That, against all evidence to the contrary, predators get poisoned all the time and it was just Moonburrow's turn. It was a tragedy, and I feel awful for his friends, family, and close packmates, but just because he died, that didn't mean that the rest of us needed to be on our guard.

I wanted so desperately to believe that, and I was able to do so until mid-morning on Tuesday.

Business has finally gone back to normal. I have my regulars—including Frannie, who side-eyes the chocolate chip cookie sample I put out this morning as though worried it would affect her the same way at the Can't Resist Cupcakes—and a few curious supes who stop by to gawk at me. From what Max said yesterday, the investigation is his top priority, but it's a *pack* priority.

Translation: keep my adorable snout of it.

He even tried to distract me with kisses. And, okay, it takes two to kiss so I'm not innocent for letting him attempt it, but if he thinks that he can use my not-so-fake attraction to him against me so that I stop snooping on my own... he's wrong. He wants to find out who killed Declan. I want to find out who tried to frame me with the cupcake, and who might be targeting my mate. We don't have to work together. I'm still going to do my best to figure out what's going on in Moonburrow.

First? I had to make it up to Gus. While he found the kiss amusing, he was still notably peeved that I went to the prey circle without him.

That's the best thing about being an opossum shifter. After we went upstairs, I switched shapes, going to my fur, and curled up with Gus to assure him that I'm looking out for him. He's my sidekick, my little bud, and I'm just doing my best to protect him.

He was a little snappish this morning after I got up, got showered, and got dressed. Once I was done with prep—and the grocery order I placed this morning during opening arrived—I made him an apology on a plate: chopped up egg whites and pieces of overpriced, out-of-season watermelon.

I set it down in front of him on the back counter. He dives into it.

I scratch the space between his ears. "You're spoiled, you know that?"

Gus chitters smugly, forgiveness finally achieved, right before he starts nomming on a watermelon cube.

I smile. I don't know what I'm going to do about that freak kiss last night, that spark, that attraction... that moment when the world seemed right because I was with my mate and Max almost seemed to recognize that I was his... faking it is getting a lot harder.

He said forget it.

I wish I could.

Since I can't, I do the next best thing. Like always, I throw myself into my work—and my eavesdropping. I didn't have that much hope that a stray mention about a rat who deals in wolfsbane would actually mean something, but I had hoped a little. So it didn't pan out. Now that my customers aren't treating me like a prospective murderer, maybe one of them will slip up and I'll overhear another possible lead.

In a way, I do. At least, I find out that Declan's murder being a one-and-done is probably not the case —and I find out in the most dramatic way possible.

Roxy bursts into Dough You Believe in Magic, her eyes vividly brighter, her hands thrown out in front of her. She's wearing her worn leather jacket again, over a ripped t-shirt that says 'you should see the other guy' in red letters, and she's paler than usual.

"Abigail Cloverfield is dead."

I blink. I was in the middle of rolling cookie dough and placing it on a tray. I plop the greasy ball in my hands somewhere that might be the counter, might be the tray, then reach for the damp rag I kept nearby.

Abigail Cloverfield. Hang on—

"The sweet doe shifter with the freckles?"

"One and the same, Hon. I just heard it from Leo Halloway."

I shake my head. I don't know who that is.

"You know him. Tall. Pale blond hair. He's a wolf, high-up in the pack, does something in law enforcement with the Alpha. Like a glorified meter-maid or something. He snarls when you don't pay for street parking, but is a pretty chill guy otherwise."

Oh, wait. I know him. "He stops by the bakery every week or so. Has a sweet tooth." I think back. "Likes everything with lemon in it."

I do my best to avoid him. While I was trying to stay off Max's radar, I instinctively shied away from anything 'wolf'. I think he might've been here during the catastrophe with the truth cupcakes last week, though so much of the panic of realizing that I'd charmed my customers accidentally has made my memories a little hazy.

Roxy shrugs. "Maybe. I don't know. But I was crossing down Maple, heading for my shop, when I saw him talking to someone. A witch, maybe? I don't know. She wasn't a shifter, and that's all I care about. Being curious—"

"Nosy," I mutter, still stunned that the doe I met yesterday is somehow dead now.

Roxy ignores me which, considering I want to hear the rest of her story, is probably for the best. "I decided to find out what was going on that had a wolf and witch gabbing this early. Leo heard it from the sheriff station. Abigail is dead.

"She didn't go in to work this morning. That wasn't like her. She's like you, Honey. Up at the crack of dawn, working before the rest of her office. She was some kind of lawyer, and her secretary went to her house to make sure she was okay. She sure as fuck wasn't."

"What happened?"

"She was slumped over her table, a half-empty mug of tear or some shit next to her." Roxy gives me a meaningful look. "Her lips were blue."

"Poison," I breathe out.

I don't pretend that I don't know what 'blue lips' could mean, or be shocked that *Roxy* knows. Screw her owning some kind of junk shop. The more I see the way she moves around the town, the more I'm convinced that Roxy has her dexterous raccoon fingers in every bit of Moonburrow.

Too bad she doesn't have any idea who killed Declan—or, when I ask if they have any suspicions about Abigail's murder, the doe shifter.

"I just wanted to let you know," Roxy adds after dashing my hopes that she might want to join me in mystery-solving. "Some weird shit's going down in Moonburrow, and I don't like the idea of you being mixed up in it. Be careful."

"I didn't know you cared that much." It's part tease, part wonder, and all automatic since my head is spinning with everything Roxy said.

"It's nice to have a touch of home here in Moonburrow." She shoots her finger at me, her claws at least three inches long and painted the same shade of red as the letter on her shirt. "Don't read too much into it, Morgan."

Yeah, yeah. I love you, too, Roxy.

She leaves, and I think back to last night. Abigail... she was so happy and full of life, talking about her predator mate, and the way she gave me a sachet of tea to welcome me to the prey circle—

Wait a second.

Abigail gave me tea. Roxy said she was poisoned, and there was a half-empty mug of tea found next to her. I mean, it would be nuts to think that this whole mystery revolves around little ol' me, but what if...

Screw it. Better to be safe than sorry.

Gus lifts his head, cocking it slightly when I start pulling open drawers behind the counter. Where did I put it? I made a mental note not to lose it, but of course I don't remember which drawer I shoved it in, and— *yes*! I found it!

I grab the white rectangle shoved under a pile of local take-out menus. Mumbling the numbers out loud as I dial them into my phone, I tap the card against the counter, waiting for it to ring.

Ring—

Ring—

"Max Lobo."

Thank goodness. I fling the card, pacing back and forth as I try to work off some of my anxious energy— and after what Roxy said, trying Abigail's tea is *definitely* out of the question. "Max, hi. It's Honey. Listen. You said to call if I'm scared. Well, I'm not. At least, I don't think I am. More concerned, but... okay. It's about Abigail. I—"

The bell over my front door jingles as Max shoves it in with his right hand. His left is clutching his phone tightly, holding it to his ear, listening to me as I ramble.

Like an idiot, I stare at him while speaking into my own. "Oh. You're here."

He nods, and I disconnect the call before placing mine down on the counter. I miss. Too distracted by the solemn expression twisting Max's rugged features, I don't even know where the counter really is. The phone clatters on the floor.

Claws crossed that I didn't just smash the screen.

Gus lifts his head. He'd curled up again when Roxy left, though I should've known better than to think he fell asleep. Climbing out of his flour bag throne, his tail slithering behind him, he scurries down the edge of the counter, using the supply drawer handles as a ladder before he hops done, using his snot to scoot the phone over to me.

"Thanks, Gus," I murmur. Squatting down, I grab the phone with one hand. With the other, I heft Gus up, giving him an elevator ride back to his perch.

Max is still standing in the doorway, silent as the grave and just as imposing.

Talk about déjà vu. I feel like we're thrown back to... jeez, it hasn't been a week yet... to less than a week ago when I woke up to question marks in his eyes.

That's accusation there. That's suspicion.

Ah, crud.

"I didn't do it!"

He holds up his empty hand. When he speaks, his

voice is more gentle than I've ever heard him be. The look has fled from his gaze as quickly as I noticed it. "Take it easy, Killer. I know you didn't."

You know what? I might have an easier time believing him if he didn't insist on calling me 'Killer' like that. I'm not sure how that went from a distracted nickname to an... I don't know... term of endearment almost, but after last night's kiss, it has... and that has me even more nervous than before.

Which explains why, instead of being grateful that he's not here to arrest me for Abigail's murder, I simply ask him, "How?"

Long legs eat up the distance between us in seconds. His pine scent wraps around me, and I gaze up at him, exhaling softly.

"Did you do it, Honey?" he asks, his voice calm and direct. He's an Alpha. No shifter can resist submitting to the quietly-stated dominance in his tone. "Did you poison Declan? Did you kill Abigail?"

I look him right in the eyes. "No," I say softly.

He leans over the counter, rubbing the side of his thumb against the height of my cheek. "That's how I know."

I squeal. I want nothing more than to lean into his unexpected caress, but after last night, I know that's a terrible, terrible idea. Forget it, Honey. As long as we're solving murders here, you have to *forget* it.

I duck out of his reach, brushing my braid out of my face, letting it settle behind my shoulder. "Oh. Okay. But then why..."

"Am I here?" His nostrils flare slightly. "I scent raccoon. Roxy Kane?"

I nod.

"I figured. Did she tell you about Abigail Cloverfield? Is that how you knew?"

The way he asks the question, I'm pretty sure Max already knows the answer. "Yes."

It's his turn to nod. "Right. Well. It's true. I just came from her house."

And he came here? "Did you find out what happened? Roxy said it might be poison, but... any clues or scents or—"

"Peppermint," he says flatly. "I brought my best noses. None of us could catch anything but peppermint."

Peppermint and blue lips. Unless we have a copycat, it's the same person who killed Declan.

"I just stopped by to make sure you're keeping out of it like I told you. But you... you were already calling me." A muscle ticks in his cheek. "What's wrong?"

He wants me to keep out of it. If my suspicions are correct, that might not be as easy as the sheriff telling me what to do.

"Hang on. I want to give you something."

"Honey—"

"Two seconds," I tell Max, holding up a pair of fingers. "Gus, watch the bakery. I'll be right back."

Taking his job as my guard opossum seriously, Gus clambers out of his basket and hops onto the top of the pastry display. He rears up on his hind legs, staring at Max. If he could, he'd be putting his little claws on his flank, warning the predator to watch it.

Hey. I'd much rather Gus try to intimidate Max than the wolf shifter growling softly and making Gus keel over, playing dead. The more Max tolerates my sidekick, the more I find myself softening toward him, and since that's a bad idea right now... I flash him a grin.

"Two second," I echo, then hurry through the swinging doors leading to the kitchen.

I don't stay in the kitchen long. I head for the stairs, scampering up them, an opossum in her skin, until I'm rushing to search for my purse. Once I have the tiny pink sachet in hand, I race downstairs, returning to the bakery in time to catch Max rubbing Gus's pointed snout, my supposed 'guard' humming softly at the touch.

I clear my throat. Max is an Alpha. No way he couldn't sense me coming back, scent-dampener spell or not. He wanted me to see, and that's something to think about at a different time.

Leaning over the counter, I hold out the sachet.

Max frowns.

"Go on. Take it. But be careful. Use the strings."

He does. "Why are you giving me this?"

"Because Abigail gave it to me," I tell Max. "And because I think it might be poisoned."

CHAPTER 11
PROTECTIVE CUSTODY

I don't know how Max's chemist buddy is able to analyze the tea so quickly, but just as I'm closing up the bakery for the night, I see flashing lights reflecting blue and red in my store window. My heart stops. I reach for my phone, just in case, hand on my chest when Max parks his cruiser on the side of the street. He leaps out, jogging to the door.

I'm already scurrying around the side of the

counter, racing to the door to unlock it before he can even form the fist he'll use to bang on the glass.

I yank it open. "Max?"

"You're coming with me."

What? "Why?"

"Because your instincts were spot-on, Honey. The tea you gave me was poisoned. It had silver in it. Wolfsbane. Chamomile and nightroot powder."

Chamomile makes sense. Like Abigail said, it helps with nerves. Nightroot powder is a little different. My grandmother has a very small jar of it. Deep violet when the normally blue leaves are ground down, just a pinch is enough to activate 'dream' spells. I don't mess with those. I'm only a quarter-witch, and they are well out of my league. Dream spells are a supe's answer to human drugs. They lift you up, and if the witch casting the spell knows what they're doing, they're harmless; if the witch doesn't, the crash is brutal.

A tea with those four ingredients would have you smiling and at peace as you shuffle your way off the mortal coil so long as you're a supe. One mug means death.

In Abigail's case, not even a full mug did.

And she gave *me* a sachet.

Did she mix this herself? She was a doe shifter, but I know better than anyone that you can appear to be one thing while being something else. I faked being a full witch for months when I'm three-quarters opossum. Maybe Abigail had witchblood, too, but if she did? It didn't save her.

If I was a tea drinker, it wouldn't have saved me, either.

"I didn't make that. I mean, Abigail gave it to me last night. She said it would help with the nerves that prey shifters get living in a town full of predators."

"Nerves?" Max cocks his head slightly. "Do *I* make you nervous, Killer?"

Yes, but not in the way he thinks—especially when he growls a little as he calls me by that nickname. Since this is the worst possible moment to mention that, I shake my head. "I didn't plan on drinking that tea. Not a florally tea person here." And even if it didn't have a strong scent—thank you, wolfsbane—I'm still not really a fan of chamomile... or *dying*. "If I knew it was poisoned... I would've told Abigail not to drink it, either. But she said she *made it*."

"If she made it, she must have known it was poison," Max muses, letting me off the hook when it comes to answering his question. "But she drank it."

"Doesn't mean she wanted to. Doesn't mean someone didn't swap out a clean batch for poison."

He nods, thinking over my suggestion—and then he frowns. "But she would've still tried to poison you if she hadn't."

Yeah. It's kind of hard to deny that part.

"And that's why you're coming with me."

I don't understand. "But I didn't do it! You can't arrest me."

Max firms his jaw. "I'm not arresting you. I'm taking you into protective custody."

PROTECTIVE CUSTODY, AS IT TURNS OUT, MEANS BEING ferried away to the heart of Moonshadow Pack land, and given a spare bedroom in Max's Alpha cabin.

He gave me a minute to argue before pulling the Alpha card. He doesn't even go straight to being Sheriff Lobo. He's Max, the most powerful wolf in Moonburrow, and if he wants to keep me safe, he's going to keep me safe. His wolf insisted on it, and when his dominance poured off of him, I didn't even bother to keep up the fight.

Instead, I made it a point to tell him that Gus was coming with me—Max smartly didn't push back on *that*—before saying we'd need ten minutes to pack everything we would need for an extended stay. I thought about reminding him that I would need to be back at work tomorrow at five in the morning, but I decided that I would keep that surprise to myself.

I should've known better. By the time I had packed two small overnight bags—one with a couple of changes of clothes and toiletries for me, another with everything Gus might need—Max had scrawled a note on a scrap of paper he found before taping it to my front door.

By order of the sheriff of Moonburrow, Dough You Believe in Magic will be closed until further notice.

I'd quirked any eyebrow at him, clamping my teeth together.

He crossed his arms over his chest. "This way nobody in town thinks that you're another victim."

Oh, no. But they'll sure as hell figure out that the sheriff has a vested interest in me. For good or for bad, I'm not staying off anybody's radar anymore.

Go Honey. Whee!

I tried not to pout too much as Max drove Gus and me toward the far edges of Moonburrow. Gus sat on my lap, both curious and wary. I haven't figured out what Gus thinks of Max yet, though I remember the way that Gus was letting Max pet him.

Hm. Maybe my sidekick was showing me a hint of his approval, too.

I honestly didn't believe that Max was really going to put us up in his actual cabin. That's... I know enough about a wolf pack that what he's insisting on... it's unusual.

An Alpha cabin is more than just a house for the pack leader. It's a symbol of his position at the top of the pack. Wolves think of their hierarchy as a triangle. The Alpha is the point at the top. Next comes the Beta, followed by Gammas, the older enforcers that have retired after protecting the pack. Deltas make up the bulk of a wolf pack; they're the rank-and-file members with varying levels of dominance.

In Moonburrow, there is one final tier: everyone else. Specifically, prey shifters and witches, since no matter how powerful we might be in our own ways, the wolves will always see us as weaker than them.

All Alpha cabins are basically split in two, and his is no exception. One side belongs to Max and only Max; the only exception being, of course, his invited guests. It's his private territory, and to encroach on it is basically a challenge to his authority as Alpha. We don't have many challenges among opossums. With the adrenaline ramping up too high, we tend to drop before finishing a fight, so an opossum challenge would be pretty anticlimactic.

Wolf challenges? Predators? They're a completely different story. Mercy is a rarity. To let your opponent walk away, it's a sign that an Alpha won't do whatever he must to hold his seat. If you can't trust an Alpha to quash a challenger, it's easy to start second-guessing whether he'll protect you when it counts. Eventually, even if the first challenger gives up, there will be plenty more to take their place.

So, yeah. No one goes in that side of the cabin. The smaller half, however, is what they refer to as the pack den. It's a place where all packmates can go and petition Max for whatever help they need. That's communal space, and I figured he would set me and Gus up on a spare couch in the den all the way up until he helps us out of the cruiser, leading us to the front door on the larger half.

I drag my feet. It doesn't work. His hand is on my shoulder, giving me the subtle nudge I need to take the path toward his entrance.

He shoves in the door. It's not locked. Of course it's not. Who would even think about trying to rob the Alpha?

I gulp, clutching Gus to me. He squeaks when I squeeze him harder than I should. Murmuring an apology under my breath, I loosen my hold, then peer up at Max. "And this is okay?"

He keeps his other hand where it is, guiding me inside. "I'm the Alpha. I want you here. That's all that matters."

A shiver jerks down my spine.

"It's alright, Killer. You're safe here. As long as you're under my protection, no one can get to you."

It takes everything I have to keep all of my blood from rushing to my face. I'm a prey shifter. Letting a predator—letting an Alpha—be responsible for my safety is part of the gig. But it's not just any predator, it's my fated mate, and he's leading me into *his* house.

I haven't felt like I was going to faint in days, and while I manage to stay standing, it's a little touch and go for a second there.

The house smells of Max. Of pine and richness, a masculine musk and *mine*. The cabin is decorated to suit him: everything is in shades of chocolate, something that soothes my baker's heart.

Doing my best to ignore that, I turn to him. "Do I really need protection?"

"There's a murderer on the loose."

I quirk my lips in a crooked grin. "Are you sure you didn't just invite her into your territory?"

The look he gives me has my knees turning to jelly. "Yes, Honey. I'm sure."

Oh. I blink. My knees are weak, but they're not really wobbly. Not like I'm about to play possum. I'm still on my feet, and if my inner beast had her way, I'd be sleeping in *Max*'s bed tonight.

I shake my head. Right. Spare guest room. "So where should I—"

A knock raps against the thick wooden door. Max was already turning to unlock it, his senses giving him an advance warning that we were about to have a guest.

As he tugs in the door, I peek around Max.

Standing on the porch, wearing another expensive-looking silk shirt and pressed trousers set, is Riordan, the Moonburrow deputy and Moonshadow Pack Beta.

He nods at Max. "The pack council is waiting for you."

IF IT WAS BAD ENOUGH THAT I WAS GOING TO HAVE TO sleep in the Alpha cabin tonight, add that to being told that my presence was expected at the pack meeting next door.

There were at least ten different wolves waiting for Max and Riordan to join them. I slipped in, hoping that all of the predators wouldn't notice the two prey animals—one wild, one a shifter—among them. Yeah, right. I had shifter eyes flashing at me from all directions.

Gus is on my shoulder. I reach up, laying my palm on his rump, comforting both of us as I shuffle to the other side of the room.

It's much less furnished than the Alpha cabin. I see one large desk tucked near the back of the room, a seat behind it, and two seats in front of it. Max takes the seat behind the desk. No one sits in the visitor's chairs. I almost do, but figure putting a little distance between me and Max might be a better idea right now.

Once he's sitting, he gets right to business.

Gesturing at each of the wolves in turn, he gives me a name and rank as though we're part of the human military and not a shifter pack. They each nod—to Max, not me—and I wonder what the hell is going on.

Until he gets to the last one, and I'm suddenly distracted.

"And, of course, you've already met Riordan Lobo, Pack Beta."

Lobo.

Lobo.

"Riordan's your brother?" I blurt out. "I thought he was the Beta."

"Yes. I just said that."

Duh. "And the deputy."

"He is."

But he's his *brother*?

I turn on him, trying to look past the slick facade.

Max doesn't like it. "What are you staring at?"

"You're making me blush," Riordan deadpans.

I want to hush them both as I focus. Instead, I say almost distractedly, "He's handsome—"

Yeah. Wrong thing to say because, suddenly, Max growls and the tension in the air cranks up.

Crap. "No." I smile over at the Alpha before I think better of it. "You're handsome, too, Max."

"Max?" Riordan raises his eyebrows. "Getting friendly with the suspect, are you?"

"She's not a suspect," he snaps, glaring at his brother. "She's in protective custody."

I'm almost choking on the sudden testosterone filling the air. Phew.

The rest of the wolves are smart enough to keep out of it. You think I would be, too.

Nah.

"Okay. I'm trying to figure this out." I point at Max, then Riordan, then Max again. "Who's older?"

Riordan juts out his chin. "Me."

And he's an alpha wolf. A dominant alpha wolf. He buries it well, especially when he's next to Max, but if he's any less dominant than his younger brother, I'll walk around with Gus's beloved bag of flour on my head and call it my new hat.

I screw up my face, trying to figure it out.

To my right, Max's growl turns into a snarl.

What the—

I leap back, heart thudding wildly as my head shoots over to the normally stoic sheriff. He has fangs out, claws on display. His eyes are more of a molten lava than dark gold, his wolf riding him so hard, it's like he's seconds away from shifting on the spot.

He's losing control. I was focusing on his brother, and Max looks like he wants to rip out his throat.

My leap backward helps. Putting some distance between me and Riordan does enough to keep Max in his seat. He clears his throat, but it doesn't matter. He snarled and we all heard it.

He snarled, like a protective wolf warning other males away from his mate.

Uh-oh...

If that realization isn't bad enough, Gus suddenly jumps off of his perch on my shoulder, landing with a soft *thump* as he hits the wooden floor. Quick as a flash, he moves through the gathering of predators like a shark slicing through the ocean.

With the rest of the wolves watching, Gus hooks his tiny claws in Max's jeans, climbing up his leg, jumping off of his thigh, and landing expertly in the middle of his desk. Then, whirling around, he rears up and starts chittering in warning at Max.

Huh. I guess Gus isn't a big fan of seeing Max's jealousy. Me... I'm all for it, but I don't think I'd like to see how the Alpha will react when a wild opossum starts chewing him out.

I take a step forward.

"If that creature had thumbs, I'd think it would stab you, Max," remarks Riordan with obvious interest.

I hurry the rest of the way toward the desk.

Gus shows his hind foot to Max, then swishes his tail. Yes, bud. I know opossums have opposable thumbs on their rear feet, plus a prehensile tail that's perfectly capable of wrapping around a small knife.

Given the right motivation, I think my sidekick would totally stab my mate.

I scratch his chin before scooping him up, cradling him against my sweater. "Remember, Gus, we're guests here."

Or prisoners. I'm not so clear on that part yet.

"You're also in danger," Max reminds me. "Moonshadow, this is Honey Morgan. And I hold each and every one of you responsible for making sure she's not the third murder in Moonburrow."

CHAPTER 12
CHOCOLATE CHIP COOKIE DOUGH

After my introduction, Riordan brings me back to Max's personal side of the cabin. Before, I thought he was doing his duty as the Beta. Now? It makes a lot more sense that he's Max's brother, even if I don't quite understand why the older brother is content to take a backseat, letting his younger brother rule the pack.

He doesn't seem surprised at all when I mention that Max said I would be using the spare bedroom in the Alpha cabin. He grabs the two bags that I left abandoned in the front room, showing me to a very pristine, slightly musty room that has probably never seen a guest. It's clean, but clearly unused, and Riordan tells me to make myself at home. Once the pack meeting is over, Max will be right back to talk to me.

He's right. I have enough time to unpack our few belongings, check out the bathroom attached to my room, and give Gus some of the cat kibble I keep on hand for a quick meal. My stomach is growling. I ignore it. It's well past the time I usually have my dinner, and when I swear I smell food drifting in through the open door, I'm sure I'm imagining it.

I'm not.

"Killer? You dead?"

I snort to myself, a sliver of relief flashing through me when I recognize Max's voice. In a cabin that radiates *Max* everywhere, drenched in his intoxicating scent, it's hard for me to track him. He's here now, though, and when me and Gus join him in the living room only to find that the source of the delicious food is coming from a stuffed bag in his hand, I can't help myself.

"Oh, Max. I love you."

His eyebrows shoot so high, they nearly disappear in his hairline.

I play back my words and nearly drop from embarrassment.

Waving my hands, I say, "No. Not like that. I just... Food. You have food."

"I usually cook, but things have been... well, hectic is a nice way to put it. I didn't think it was safe to order out when we have a poisoner in town, but I called my mother. She still likes to take care of her pups no matter how grown we are. I already gave Riordan his plate. If you don't mind that I'm feeding you... or Anne Lobo is... I'd like to share a meal with you, Honey."

How can I say no?

He's not propositioning me. Unlike me, Max has totally been able to forget our kiss. He's just doing his duty. He's the sheriff... he's the *Alpha*. He's looking out for me, and part of that is making sure that I don't starve on his watch.

True, it's hard to convince myself of that when he doles out perfectly seared steak, buttery mashed potatoes, steamed carrots, and fresh-baked rolls onto a plate for each of us. He has a cozy four-seater table in his kitchen. Max takes one seat. From the position where he places my plate, he wants me sitting opposite him.

Gus—unwilling to be left out again—plops himself in the middle of the table, glancing between Max and me.

However, as soon as he starts asking me questions in between eating his meal, I start to get suspicious. Talking about the bakery is one thing, asking me about

Virginia and Roxy is another, but then he turns the topic to the prey circle meeting I attended and warning bells start to go off in my head.

I take a bite of my delicious steak, chew, then poise my fork over my potatoes. "Is this an interrogation, sheriff?"

"Maybe I just want to get to know my new house-guest better."

"You can tell me. Afraid you invited a serial killer under your roof?"

A small grin turns his rugged face from handsome to damn near irresistible. "I'm an Alpha. I'm not afraid of anything."

I don't know what it was that he said, or how Gus even understood him enough to be offended, but my little buddy suddenly launches himself at Max. You'd think an Alpha would be able to stop him in time. Nope. Suddenly Gus is sinking his teeth into the first knuckle on the pointer finger on Max's left hand.

I jump up from my seat, fork clattering against my plate. "Gus!"

"I stand corrected," Max says, chuckling softly as he gently disengages Gus's jaw from around his finger. It's still attached, thank goodness, even if he's bleeding. "Opossums can be very terrifying. Thank you for reminding me of that, Gus."

Gus chitters, then scampers back to his earlier position—and Max lets him.

I lose a little more of my heart to Max Lobo then and there.

Some predators would react on instinct. A prey animal challenging them? Attacking them? *Biting* them? They would've picked Gus up, shook him a couple of times, and that would be the end of my beloved sidekick. He already gave Gus a pass in the den. This might be taking it too far.

But Max... his knuckle surprisingly still bleeding, he sneaks a piece of carrot off his plate, giving it to the opossum.

And I have to admit that I don't have that much more heart left to give before the curious sheriff has it all.

Hours later, I'm lying in my borrowed bed, in the middle of a dream that involves Max, me, and a whole lot of chocolate chip cookie dough.

"Oh, *Max...*" I mumble. In my dreams I don't have to pretend that I'm not addicted to him. "You taste so *good...*"

Something touches my face.

I swipe at it, still half asleep. I don't want to leave my dream.

There it is again. Chilly and damp and—

I slap my cheek, turning away, hoping that I can cling to sleep.

Nope. Something *tickles* me now and, yup, that's it for me.

I open my eyes and look straight into a beady pair of eyes and a twitching pink nose. The whiskers on the left side of his snout are brushing up against my cheek, stealing the last of my dream away.

Not Max.

Gus.

I jerk back, landing hard on the mattress. So hard, in fact, that I send my poor sidekick flying. He goes *whee*, a few inches into the air, before landing on his side, all four legs kicking out as he tries to right himself.

"Gus? Oh my goodness, *Gus*. You know better than to get so close to my face when I'm sleeping."

I instinctively trust Gus. My inner opossum would never see him as a threat. If he spooks me while I'm fast asleep, I won't wake up and immediately faint. I'll react instead, which is exactly what happened.

I reach for my bewildered opossum. He clicks his teeth together, dashing away from me.

Frowning, I murmur his name.

He goes to the foot of the bed where he rears back on his hind legs, sitting up. His tail curls around his back paws. Chittering wildly, he lifts one of his right paws, undeniably gesturing at the window.

My head turns, searching for what he wants to show me—and I freeze.

Someone is looking at me. It's a silhouette against the glass, but the fierce, glowing gold eyes tell me that it's a wolf shifter in his skin peering at me while I slept.

I scream. As loud as I possibly can, to wake up the nearby pack, to scare off the peeping tom, I scream.

Later, I'll wonder why that was my reaction. Why, when faced with a pair of wolfish eyes staring through the glass at me, I didn't immediately keel over like I always used to. That's been what I do my whole life. Not tonight. As though my inner beast knew that we had a predator to protect us while we stay conscious, I scream—and, barely ten seconds later, the guest room door swings in as Max storms through it.

He went to bed in a pair of sleep pants. I get my first look at his sculpted chest, the way sleep musses his soft hair, and how there's a slight crease in his cheek from a wrinkle in his pillowcase.

Max looks exactly like what he is: a male who got ripped out of sleep. At the same time, there's something in the way his body is hunched slightly, drawing my attention to his furless chest, his toned body, and the absolute dominance pouring off of him.

His eyes seem to gleam in the dark of the bedroom, a glowing orange that tells me that I'm looking at the Alpha in all his glory.

"What's wrong?" he snarls, his fury for whatever—whoever—made me scream. "I heard you scream."

I point at the window. "Wolf shifter. Peeking into the room. I saw him!"

Do I know that it's a *him*? No, but the height and the... I don't know... *vibe* I got makes me convinced that it was a male out there, and he wasn't just being a perv because I'm a female.

Max obviously agrees. "I'll go see if I can run him down. You two stay here."

An Alpha can order members of his pack, expecting them to obey. A mate might make suggestions, but in an equal partnership, he should hope that his mate has a brain.

Poor Max. He's stuck with Honey Morgan.

I point at Gus. "Stay here," I tell him, then pause only long enough for the power of Max's dominance to fade. Once I'm sure he's outside of the cabin, searching for whoever was spying on me, I shut my door behind me to keep Gus in, then take off after him in my pajamas.

They're cute. A matching shirt and pants combo with red cherries all over the pink material, I'm thinking that I probably should've changed into something dark if I wanted to hide in the woods. As it is, anyone seeing the blonde prey shifter running through the trees will know exactly who I am, whether I try to hide in the shadows or not.

I try to use my sniffer to scent him. Not happening. The entire Alpha cabin and its territory smells so strongly like Max, it's impossible to pick up any other scent.

So I decide to go around the cabin, heading toward the outside of my borrowed bedroom. It has to be the point where Max started to search for whoever was out there, and if I'm probably being a ding-dong, running *toward* the creep... I go anyway.

Nothing. There are footsteps standing directly in front of my window—and I wave at Gus through the glass so that he knows I'm okay—but I don't see anyone.

I don't *see* anyone.

I *hear* them.

A low, throaty howl rips through the night. For a second, I stiffen, but as though it was a song meant for my soul, I'm not afraid of the wolf singing it. The opposite, really. I go running for him.

I find him, too. About fifty yards from the cabin, I stop short when an oversized wolf comes padding toward me.

I swallow a sudden lump in my throat. "Max? Is that you?"

It has to be. My normal reaction to seeing a wolf—whether it was a shifter or wild—would be to play dead. Duh. But when I see this beautiful creature with the russet-colored fur so similar to Max's hair, plus a pair of gleaming, golden, *intelligent* eyes... *Max*'s eyes... I know it has to be him.

He's a gorgeous wolf. Of course he is. He's a gorgeous male in his skin. I expect no less of him when he's shifted.

Max stops when he sees me. I can just imagine the human version of Max gritting his teeth, a muscle jerking in his cheek as he accepts that I did the opposite of what he ordered me to do.

The big wolf shudders. A split second later, his body changes. A shift is like a snap. It's one of your shapes remembering that it exists, taking over from the other. We're supes. Even if we can't cast spells like witches, any supernatural creature is touched by magic. There's magic inherent to every shift. The force of it is enough to blow off anything we're wearing that isn't enchanted to survive the blast.

That's why shifters try to take off their shoes and clothing before they shift. If they don't, the shift inevitably destroys them, the material turning to ruined tatters. We're naked as our beasts. We return naked when we go from four legs to two.

I know that. I've been a shifter my entire life. I've been caught without a change of clothes more times than I want to admit, and for half of those occasions, I have Roxy to blame. Same for the countless amount of times I fainted because she thought it would be hilarious to startle me...

Nudity isn't a big deal for shifters. I knew what a penis looked like before I knew what a penis *was*. The only time it carries a different weight is when sexual attraction is involved.

And, oh, I've been attracted to Max Lobo for months now.

He shifts, and it isn't until he's standing in front of me without a stitch on that I really appreciate how beautiful a nude male's body can be. From the cut of his muscles to his tapered waist to the cock that's stirring slightly from the adrenaline of the chase, Max is stunning... he's naked...

He isn't mine.

Not yet.

I squeal, and though it's considered bad form to draw attention to a shifter being bare when you have clothes on, I can't help it. I cover my eyes.

"Honey—"

"You're naked."

Max ignores that. "What are you doing out here? I told you to stay in the cabin."

He did. And if I had, I wouldn't be standing here with my cheeks flaming. "I wanted to help."

"Help. *Help.*" Max makes a frustrated sound in the back of his throat, followed by a sigh. "I told you—"

"Are you covered yet?"

To my surprise, Max lets out a barking laugh. "What are you, twelve?"

"Twenty-eight, and you're the Alpha. Tell me you have emergency stores of a change of pants or something tucked along your territory. You must. You'd never let anyone catch you vulnerable."

An Alpha wouldn't... so why did Max purposely shift in front of me? Because he wanted to talk... or because he *knows*?

"Max—"

"Don't move. I mean it this time, Honey. *Don't move.*"

I've already pushed my luck once. "Okay," I say meekly, eyes still covered.

The air shifts, the wind blowing his scent around me. I should just look. By shifting in front of me, he was giving me permission to ogle all I wanted so long as I kept my paws to myself. I should look...

I drop my hand, not sure how I feel when I see that Max is gone. Nervous, definitely. Disappointed? Maybe.

Where did he go?

"Max?"

He reappears, his bottom half covered with a basic pair of grey sweatpants. Ah, grey sweatpants... I can still see an impressive dick imprint against the fabric, but at least I can pretend I can't.

"Better?" he rumbles, a hint of pure grump in his tone.

Not really. I didn't mind getting a peek at all Max

had to offer, but it wasn't fair. Maybe if he knew we were fated to be mates, I could've finally stopped pretending like I haven't been drawn to him for months now. I want him. I care for him. If he keeps doing everything he can to keep me from becoming *dead* dead, I could see myself admitting that I *love* him... but that's not fair to either of us to drop that bomb in the middle of a murder investigation.

So I don't. I don't answer him, either.

I just look up at him with trust and hope. "Did you find the guy?"

Max scowls.

My heart sinks.

Not even the Alpha could track down an interloper on his territory. What the fuck does that mean?

Unless...

Unless it wasn't an interloper.

Unless it was a packmate who knows this land as well as Max does.

It's possible, and I just hope like hell that this was a freak occurrence, that it doesn't have anything to do with Declan's murder.

One look at the way Max's expression closes off to see my hopes dash tells me: keep dreaming, Honey.

Where's the chocolate chip cookie dough when you need it?

Ah, how cute. He doesn't even know that we could be mated one day, but already we've had our first spat as an almost-couple.

Max wanted to send me right back to the cabin. He even pulled the Gus card, asking me if I wouldn't feel better if I could assure myself that the face I saw in the window hadn't double-backed and gone after my opossum once I'd chased after Max.

I told him the truth. I told him that, now that he put the idea in my head, I was going back for Gus, but —and it was a big but—if he continued to search for clues without me, then I'd grab Gus and we'd do a little sleuthing of our own.

He pointed out that he's the Alpha and has the right to lock me in the cabin.

I smiled and said he could try. I might be a prey shifter. I'll give him that. I'm not a powerless human who will stay put because the Alpha flashed his high beams at me.

He unscrewed his jaw enough to say, "Please."

That almost did it, I admit. If I didn't care for Max, I would've folded. Only I *do* care, and maybe it was my anxiety flaring up, but I'd convinced myself that, if I wasn't there to watch Max's back, something terrible would happen.

Did I forget that he's the most powerful predator in Moonburrow? Nah. Could he have sent up another howl, gathering some of the higher-ranked wolves to join us on the search? Of course.

Did he do that?

No. I don't know why, and I wasn't about to question it. He gave in. He was still going to do a quick hunt through his immediate territory, and if I wanted to come along, I could.

And if he muttered something about at least he'll know where I am if I stay with him, I'm sure he's just taking his Alpha responsibilities super seriously…

We do go back to the cabin. We're near enough that he wants to do another check to see if the unknown wolf really *did* double-back, and I want to make sure Gus is okay. Max decided that, if I'm going to be his shadow, he would stay in his skin. He took two minutes to get fully dressed, including putting on shoes.

I went ahead and did the same, trading my pajamas for a dark green long-sleeved shirt, black leggings, my sneakers, and, ugh, even a bra.

It's harder to leave Gus behind this time, but to my surprise, it's Max who explains to my opossum that Gus needs to stay behind and hold down the fort. I swear to Fate, Gus salutes Max before positioning himself in the middle of the rumpled bed I'd been sleeping in.

Max closes the door, gives me a chance to stay behind, and huffs when I smile sweetly, telling him to lead the way.

CHAPTER 13
A DIFFERENT TYPE OF POISON

It's not very easy doing this 'sleuthing in the woods' thing when you have a six-foot tall Alpha so close up your ass, you feel like he'd climb into your skin to keep you safe. Hey. I get being overprotective. That's part of being a pack; if he wasn't concerned for a weaker packmate under his protection, he'd be a shit Alpha. Max Lobo isn't a shit anything, and right now he's doing a brilliant impression of a bodyguard.

I wish I could let myself enjoy it. That he was acting this way because he was my mate, and my safety was the most important thing in this world to him. But since I made this mess and have to wait to see it through to the end, it's getting a little frustrating.

"You don't have to keep doing that," I finally tell him when I... I just can't take it anymore.

"Doing what?"

"Hovering. Growling at twigs. Acting like I'm going to trip over my own shadow and break my neck."

He's quiet long enough that I have to wonder if he's ignoring me. Then, in a gruff voice that breaks the silence of the woods: "You might. You're a trouble magnet, Killer. If something like that does that happen, I'd rather be there when you do. Maybe I can catch you."

And maybe my heart stutters to hear him say that.

I stop, turning on my heel so that I can look at Max's profile. The hint of moonlight overhead catches the golden glint in his eye, softening his sharp features.

"It's not control, Honey," he says, voice low. "It's instinct. You walk into danger, I follow. Every damn time. If you want to follow me, I'll slow down so that you can keep the pace."

He sounds almost frustrated, like he doesn't understand why he can't keep himself from chasing after me —or letting me stay by his side while we search for a possible killer who, for all my teasing, is definitely *not* me.

"That's very nice of you," I begin, not really sure how I'm going to finish my comment.

No need. Max thrusts his hand through his hair, claws leaving track marks through the russet-colored strands. "You ever think maybe I'm not growling at you? Maybe I'm growling at the idea of you getting hurt."

Oof. That's a guilty pang running through me right there.

This is my fault. What started out as a way to guard my heart from rejection has gone too far. It hasn't been a week since I've been thrown into this with Max—or, well, butted my nose into this murder case... though that's not really fair when the killer involved me *first*—but it feels like I've known Max my entire life. Bonded mates have forever. The two months that I've spent avoiding him while I got out of my own head... it's nothing in the grand scheme of things.

Right?

"Max—"

"They're targeting you, Honey. You're too sweet to see it." He rumbles deep in his chest. "They came onto my territory. They challenged me. I can't let that stand... I can't let you get hurt, either."

Too sweet to see that I'm in danger? Oh, I see it alright. But between running my bakery without my family finding out I'm in trouble, trying hard not to swoon as I learn more about my fated mate, our forced proximity making it impossible for me to keep up my walls around me... worrying about some deranged supe-killer is a little low on my priorities right now.

Mainly because, some time after Sheriff Lobo became *Max*, I began to trust him with my safety. Gus's safety, too, and if that doesn't say anything about the way my feelings are changing, nothing will.

Two shifters are dead. I was kind of, sort of involved in both murders, between Declan and the cupcake, plus Abigail and the tea. I'll clear my name, help Max close the case, and then I can focus on telling him that he's my mate—and maybe figure out why *he* hasn't realized that I'm *his*.

I don't know what I'm doing. My one lead crashed out; I have no clue if Max ever had the chance to talk to Joey and, if he did, I doubt the Alpha would fill *me* in. It's one thing, letting me tag along. It's another entirely for him to stand back and watch as a prey shifter bumbled around trying to do his job for him—

I blame myself. Being so close to Max is a distraction in and of itself, plus I keep thinking that we're wasting our time. Whoever was peeking at me, their eyes gave them away. They're a supe, and probably far, far away by now. I'm only going through the motions because my inner opossum likes having this quiet time with our mate.

It's selfish and it's stupid, but that doesn't stop me from forging ahead.

The snake appearing from beneath a pile of autumn leaf litter? That might... for a moment, at least.

It's a long, thick, coil of a snake with a copper-colored head and hourglass-shaped bands across its body. I heard the rustle a second before it broke out from under the damp leaves. As usual, it aims right for me.

My reflexes are usually much faster than this. On a good day, I can boot a snake away before it sinks its fangs into me. On a bad one—like tonight—I only stop it after I've been bit.

"Damn it!"

Not again. Ugh. I liked these leggings, and it's so annoying that they'll have holes from the snake's fangs in them. Larger ones now that I have to bend over, grabbing the snake, yanking it out of my skin, before tossing it about fifteen feet away from me.

It slithers off into the night while I lower myself enough to see the damage to my leggings.

Max is already reaching for me. The entire snake attack lasted less than five seconds, and for four of them, the Alpha snarled before he reacted.

Suddenly, he's at my side, barking directions. "Stay calm. I've got you. Okay? That was a fucking copperhead. It's venomous, but I'm here. We've got to wash that out. Get you to the doc. Make sure it doesn't—"

I wave him off. "I'm fine."

He stays down, his hand on my shoulder, steadying

me. "You've been bitten by a snake. A *venomous* snake. I swear to the Luna, you'll be fine... I'll make sure of it. But first—"

"Yup. Don't worry about it. I got this. I appreciate your concern, but I really am fine."

He glares at my flippant answer. "If your shifted form is anything like your pet—"

"Gus isn't my pet. He's my sidekick."

The look Max gives me tells me that he thinks the venom is already messing with my brain. "Sure. Anyway, he's small. I don't know how much of that copperhead's venom got in you, but you're small, too. A prey shifter might not die. I don't think it's gonna be pleasant... but *wait*. You're an opossum, Honey. Why aren't you dead?"

Dead?

Oh. He means why aren't I squealing because a silly snake bit me... squealing and then, true to my type of shifter, keeling over so that another snake can come along and chomp on my 'dead' body.

"Sorry. I could flop over and pretend if it makes you feel better."

"*Honey.*"

Ooh. The way he growls my name sends shivers up and down my spine.

"What?" Poor guy. I think he's actually worried for me. "Listen... opossums have some neat tricks that pass over to us shifters. We're solitary by design which is why I lived by myself... well, me and Gus... in the human world for a decade before I came here. You know about us playing dead, and I can climb a tree in my skin and my fur despite not being athletic in any other way. And we're basically immune to all snake venoms."

He's staring at me now. He was before, but that was because he was bracing himself so that he could catch me when I drop. I appreciate the thought, but the way his expression has changed... oof. That's another shiver —and one that has nothing to do with any poison.

I shrug, trying to get my wayward body under control. "Dad can explain it better, but we have this, like, protein in our blood. It totally neutralizes the venom instantly. You don't have to worry about me."

"I've been worrying about you since I got the call that we had a packmate down and I found you appearing to be dead a few feet away from the *very* dead Declan."

It's my turn to gape at Max. What the... what does *that* mean?

Before I can ask, he has a question of his own. "What about the poison that killed him and Abigail? Would you survive that if you ingested it?"

I think it over; that's better than wondering why the idea that Max Lobo is worrying over me has my stomach suddenly twisting. "No. It's really just snakes. I only know that because the damn things always find me, almost like they're trying to test if a part witch, part opossum, human-passing creature will beat their venom. For a reptile, even wild snakes are surprisingly vindictive."

I lick my finger, wiping away the blood on my ankle. The puncture wounds will be gone in no time; the look of panic mingled with amazement that broke through Max's stoic expression is going to last a whole lot longer.

Right. This is me, Max.

Is it any wonder that it's for the best that I hide the fact that we're mates for the moment? Really, I'm doing it for his sake…

He shakes his head slowly, the sliver of the moon over our heads reflected in his gold eyes.

I get to my feet, straightening. Reluctantly, so does Max. "What?"

"I'm just trying to figure out why opossums are classified as prey shifters."

Good question. "You'd have to ask the predators. They're the ones who enforce the idea that shifters exist on different levels—and that one is considered weak if they're not deemed powerful enough."

His cheeks hollow. "Honey—"

It's fine. "Come on. We're just jabbering here. What if that"—wolf… I'm positive that was a wolf—"guy is getting away just because I got a little prick?"

Max chokes. I can't tell if it was a half-laugh that

got caught in his throat or something else entirely. It doesn't matter. He chokes, and when he recovers, he flexes his jaw. "No. I think we're done."

What? "Why?"

His gaze flickers down to my ankle.

I roll my eyes. "Seriously? What are the odds that another Eastern copperhead snake will strike this late?"

Or early.

It might be early...

"Now that you tell me they have a vendetta against your type of supe, I won't risk it. Not when neither of us sensed it before it struck." Huh. He's right about that. "We're heading back."

"Max—"

"Humor me, Killer. What if one comes back, it goes for you, but bites me instead?"

Oh, that's *low*. I can either tell him that it wouldn't bother me if it did—he's an Alpha and would probably burn off the venom before it did more than sting a bit —or admit that I actually give a crap about the sheriff that I've been working so hard to avoid for months now.

Quick, Honey.

A distraction!

I turn slightly, ignoring the weight of his stare on the side of my face as he waits for my answer. I open my mouth—and then I gasp.

Max immediately freezes. "Honey?"

"Hang on— do you see that?"

I point a few feet ahead of us. I was looking for a distraction, but I think I might've actually found something. It glimmers in the sliver of moonlight shining down on the woods. No... it *glitters*.

Just like the poison someone added to my frosting glittered.

Max throws his hand out. Lifting his nose, he takes a deep breath. "A hint of caramel," he says, exhaling. "That's all I get." He looks at me. "Your scent is always a tease. Like, I get a whiff of it, then it's gone. Sometimes there's opossum. You or Gus... I'm blocked when you're near. But I should be able to smell the woods."

Just like he should've been able to catch the copperhead before it bit me...

The guilty pang in my chest becomes a stab almost too painful to ignore. I know why he's blocked: the scent-dampener charm that keeps him from using his instincts to take in my innate scent and aura. The woods, though? "You can't smell the outside?"

"I didn't... shit. I didn't even notice. I've lived in Moonburrow my entire life. I know every tree in the woods. Every bush. Every trail. My olfactory memory provides the scent... but we've been chasing a ghost the last half an hour. I don't smell anything except for a touch of you."

I know what he means. His dark pine scent has my

head swimming, but while a wild opossum has an exceptional sense of smell, my nose when I'm in my skin is less than average for a shifter. I didn't really smell anything out of the ordinary, either—and I think I know why.

I duck under Max's outstretched arm, scurrying where I swore I saw the glitter. He calls my name, but I don't stop until I'm right on top of it.

Silver glitter. A violet powder. Shattered glass that looks like it once belonged to a small vial. Look, I even see a cork stopper a few inches away. A black ash underlies most of the mess, and though I'm careful not to touch it or breathe it in, I know exactly what I'm looking at.

I'm looking at wolfsbane.

I'm looking at *poison*.

I'm looking at the reason why we just realized that neither of us it at a hundred percent...

Max comes to the same conclusion at the same time. Gripping my shoulders, he lifts me from my slight crouch easily, moving me until his body is between me and the shifter poison.

That, my friend, is what we call in the sleuthing business a *clue*. Someone is still mixing the concoction that first poisoned Declan. It wasn't just a one-time thing. They've killed twice already, and they had enough here to kill again before they... what? Dropped it?

Where did they get it from?

What were they going to do with it?

The wolf in the window—

No. Think of the poison. Is that what happened with the cupcake? Did someone dose it for some reason... to kill Max, maybe... and then Declan came back to the alley behind Dough You Believe in Magic to eat it?

I don't get it. It just doesn't make sense. Abigail drank poisoned tea at home. Why was Declan left in the alley? Why was that dumpsite important?

I don't know, but I'm going to do my best to find out.

RETURNING TO THE CRIME SCENE IS A TERRIBLE IDEA, which is how I know it's mine.

Even more amazing, Max agrees that we should go.

Okay. That's making our... discussion... sound a lot smoother than it really was. I suggested we go back to the bakery. Now. Not tomorrow, but since we were awake and I'm not going to be able to sleep again with the memory of those gold eyes watching me through the window, we go *now*.

Max said it was a good idea, but he was going to call Riordan and have him stay with me and Gus while he went with a few of his trusted wolves over to Dough

You Believe in Magic to see if he could find some sign of the poison now that we have a better idea of what it looks like when it isn't disguised as tea.

I said that it's *my* bakery.

He reminded me my grandmother actually owns the store.

I told him to bite me.

He showed me his fangs and said, "With pleasure, Killer."

There was plenty of snarling from the Alpha after that. I let my opossum side out and chittered in a perfect imitation of Gus that had Max looking at me in surprise. I glared at him. He called me cute.

I decided to shift gears. Softening my features, going as innocent as possible, I fiddled with one of my messy braids, peering up at him with a sheen over my purple eyes.

I said, "Please, Max," and even though we both know very well that I just manipulated the hell out of him, he sighed and said, "Let's go."

We take the cruiser. Because it's close to one in the morning when I had my brilliant idea, he keeps the lights and sirens off. There's no parking in the back alley—there's barely enough space for the garbage truck to pick up the dumpster—so he leaves his car in front of the bakery.

I hop out of the cruiser before he can come around and open my door for me. Max frowns—he did that the whole ride so I'm used to it—and follows me to the front door.

When he returned to the Alpha cabin for his car keys, I snagged my set so we could get into the bakery. We do, and I keep going until I'm unlocking the back door, leading Max out into the alley.

It still stinks of peppermint. While wolfsbane is essential in covering up a scent and dulling the connection between a shifter and their beast, whoever killed Declan wasn't taking any chances. They wanted him to suffer, and for anyone who came to investigate his death to not be able to use their shifter senses to do so.

But I'm not trying to use my nose. Now that we have an idea of what we're looking for, I want to see if the killer was as reckless by my bakery as he was on Max's territory. Too many shifters rely on their nose.

What about our eyes?

Our night vision is excellent. I don't even need to use a flashlight to see what I'm doing, though it's nice to have an alpha wolf shifter with me. The lingering peppermint might have him blowing air through his nose before he jerks up his t-shirt to give it a break, but it doesn't do a damn thing to dampen his impressive shifter strength.

I know instinctively where Declan died. Not because of any supernatural ability or anything. I've just relived the moment I noticed his legs sticking out, poked my head around the side of the dumpster, and found his corpse so many times that it's been etched into my brain.

"Here," I say.

Max nods in agreement.

When I first proposed taking the ride from the heart of pack land over to downtown Moonburrow, Max asked me why. I laid out my theory: that the same person who smashed a vial while we were searching for them in the woods might've been the same person who was peeking at me. With the nightroot, wolfsbane, and silver concoction left behind, odds are they had a connection to Abigail's tea *and* Declan's poisoned cupcake.

It all began at Dough You Believe in Magic. I still don't have a clue why anyone had to die, but one thing's for sure: Declan was found *here*. Whether he was killed here or moved so he'd be find behind my bakery is yet to be determined. I don't know if we'll ever know until we find the murderer. Still, I've been avoiding coming out here if I don't have to—letting the trash pile up so that I was taking multiple bags out to the dumpster instead of going out whenever I needed to—because I can't forget Declan's dead silver eyes and his blue lips.

No more avoiding. The body is gone; the pack burial over with. All that's left is the scent of spoiled Christmas in the air—and the four-inch gap beneath the dumpster from where it's lifted up on caster wheels.

Hmm.

We didn't come all this way to stare at the alley, then stare at each other. If the killer dropped one vial, what if he dropped another? What if it didn't smash?

Hey. I'm an amateur sleuth. He's the big shot detective. Fingerprints can come in handy when it comes to solving murders, and it would be amazing if we could find something that our murderer accidentally left behind.

Now, do I really think I'm going to have Max heft up the dumpster, peek under it into the shadows, and find a vial of poison like a smoking gun?

This is real life. It's not like one of those cozy mysteries with the strapping dark-haired cop hero and the cat sidekick. For one, Max is a sheriff whose hair has a tinge of red to it. For the other, my sidekick is a kickass opossum, thank you very much. And while I don't have a hope for a HEA until I find the words to tell Max that he's my mate, I'll be happy if we can solve the crime.

Too bad real life doesn't work that way.

Only sometimes it *does*.

"Max!" Excitement colors my tone. "Holy shit... Max! I see something. It's glittering."

He's standing there, holding the dumpster two feet

off the ground like it doesn't weigh a million pounds. "Like silver?"

Maybe. "I'm going to grab it. Don't drop the dumpster on me."

He grumbles. "Do you really think I would?"

I pause for a second.

No, I realize. I don't. Somehow, my lifelong nerves when it comes to being a prey shifter around predators have disappeared when it comes to *this* predator in particular.

"I trust you," I murmur, though maybe I have a few second thoughts when the dumpster groans, his arms jerking. "You good, Max?"

"Just get it and see what rolled under the dumpster."

Can do.

Going flat on my belly, I scooch under the two-foot gap Max created so that I can scoop up the glass vial in my hand. Slithering like a snake, I back up until I can go to my knees. Max waits until I'm clear before lowering the dumpster back to the asphalt.He wipes his hands against his jeans, then reaches out to me, offering to help me up.

I let him. Once I'm on my feet, I show him the vial.

It's half full. I can make out the dark wolfsbane ash, the nightroot powder, the glittering silver, and the same cork that we found in the woods. It's a different blend than the tea, just like I thought. The ratio is also different. It's much paler, the silver outweighing the rest of the components.

Makes sense. Declan's lips might've been blue due to the violet nightroot powder, but the only part of the poison that stood out under the microscope was the glittering silver. Not even the wolfsbane ash, either, until Max's chemist contact looked deeper into the mix of ingredients that killed Declan.

Because it did. The poison killed Declan.

This poison…

Holy shit. I think I'm looking at the exact murder weapon that did it.

I'm careful to hold it by the cork so that I don't accidentally get my fingerprints on it. I thought that would be enough, and maybe it would've been… if the vial didn't start glowing a vibrant green.

Magic green.

Ah, *crap.*

I just triggered a blow-back spell.

Grandma Jean is a pro at them. Just like how some witches specialize in charmed bakeries or dream spells, there are a few who make bank with protection spells. Most are designed to keep people safe. Others? They're offensive rather than defensive.

A blow-back spell is a highly offensive spell. If there's something that you're worried might get stolen, that you want to protect, you charm it with a blow-back. If the wrong person gets their hands on it, they're penalized.

I wasn't supposed to grab this vial. The caster meant it for someone else. And now I'm about to pay for it.

It all happens so fast. I recognize that I'm about to get hit with some nasty magic, but I don't have the reflexes to do anything to stop it.

I don't.

Max does.

He dives for me, grabbing the vial and flinging it away from us as the green turns neon. It's only arced about three feet when it detonates, but Max is already folding me into his arms, shielding me from the blast. He turns my face into his chest, bowing his head over mine, and braces us both as the magic explodes.

It's like some kind of powder bomb. It doesn't hurt, not really, but a shot of powder slams into us, causing Max—and, by extension, me—to stagger. He recovers quickly, lifting his head, then cursing under his breath.

I pull back, looking down at us.

Our clothes are covered in a very familiar black powder. Add in the fact that it suddenly feels like someone has stuffed both my nose and my ears with cotton, my inner opossum chittering softly as she curls up deep inside of me, too weak to do anything but nap... and, yeah. I know what this is.

"Wolfsbane."

Max's hands drop to my shoulders. "Did you get any in your mouth?"

His voice has an unfamiliar panicked edge to his growl that has me gaping up at him. "What?"

"Did you get any in your mouth, Honey? Did you ingest any?"

Oh. I shake my head. "No. You protected me from that. Max..." I don't know what to say except, "Thank you."

"When I find out who did that..." His fangs punch out, his wolf riding him dangerously hard. "I'm pretty sure it's just wolfsbane. No silver or else our skin would be burning right now. That doesn't mean we should play around with this stuff. It's already affecting me."

Me, too, but I can't bring myself to tell Max that. I wouldn't want to give him a coronary.

"Blow-back spell," I tell him instead. "It's a warning. Whoever charmed this didn't want anyone else touching it, but if they did, they didn't want to kill them outright. So they used wolfsbane to dull our senses and cut us off from our beasts."

"Magic?"

I nod.

"So it's not a shifter who is killing us."

I didn't say that.

"It could be a shifter and a witch. They could be working together," I say, shaking my shirt, trying to knock off as much of the wolfsbane as I can before admitting softly, "or they could be someone like me."

"It wasn't you, Honey," Max grates out.

I snort. "You sure? I was the one who brought us here and found it. Maybe I planted it."

"And then made the blow-back spell go off? Please. This isn't the time for teasing me, Killer. Someone could've really hurt you. If it had silver in it…"

I'd be dead. We'd *both* be dead. "I'm okay, Max." Giving in to my instincts, I go up on my tiptoes, laying my palm against his sharp jaw. "Feel a little light-headed, but I'm okay."

I don't even tell him that I'm feeling pretty human at the moment. I'm sure he's going through the same thing—worse, since he's an Alpha—but my admitting the lightheadedness is enough to have that ol' familiar muscle in his cheek jerking.

"That's the wolfsbane. We need to get it off of us."

Good idea. "We can go inside—"

"We need to get it off *now*."

Oh. Okay. "We could shift. That would get rid of it."

"I don't have any spare clothes."

That means, if Max shifts to get out of his wolfs-bane-covered clothes, he'll either have to stay in his fur or be in his skin… *naked*. I already got a glimpse of what he looks like undressed tonight. It took every-thing I had not to open my mouth and tell him that I recognize him as my mate.

If it happens again, I don't think I can.

"Do you have a washer—"

"What?"

"A washer, Killer? You have one in your apartment?"

"Yeah. A dryer, too, but—"

"Good. That'll do the job and I won't have to walk through Moonburrow naked." He takes off his shirt, rolling it into a ball so the wolfsbane is contained. He reaches for his jeans. "We're going to go to the coven, see the witches first thing in the morning. For now, we need to get this powder away from us."

He unzips his jeans. I stand there, staring in disbelief that this is happening.

That's right. I can handle magic being blast at me. A half-naked Max Lobo? That's when my brain fries.

He nods at me. "Come on. You're a shifter. I'm a shifter. The wolfsbane is on our clothes. They have to go."

Know what? I can't really argue that point—and maybe I don't want to—because that's how, against my best self-preservation skills, I end up in my bra and panties while Max strips down to a pair of dark blue boxer briefs.

Ah. It could've been worse. When he changed earlier, he could've gone commando.

Damn it. Why didn't he go commando?

Max catches me looking. He gives me a crooked yet

undeniably strained smile, eyes dipping to my cleavage before he forces them back to meet my stare. "You were so scandalized before. I thought, if something like this happened, I should at least keep some underwear on."

Scandalized. Right. Not ogling the male who's supposed to be my mate...

I hug my clothes to my chest. "So what now?"

He looks at me like the wolfsbane is affecting my brain. "We go inside before anyone sees you in your underwear."

"You are," I point out.

"And I'm the only one who's allowed to, Killer. Now get inside."

Huh. Since when is Max the possessive type?

And why does that have my cheeks heating up in a good way?

I don't know, but one thing is for sure: I go inside, and I hold open the door to invite him in.

***

THERE IS WOLFSBANE IN MY HAIR, PANIC IN MY bloodstream, a wolf in my kitchen, and it's the middle of the fucking night. This is fine. It has to be.

If it wasn't, I'd be sprawled out on the floor, doing my best impression of a corpse until my inner opossum decided that the danger had passed enough to let me come back to life.

Instead, I'm hesitating, not sure what to do next when Max calls out my name softly.

"Honey."

I glance over at him. "Yeah?"

"Did you really give Declan that cupcake for me?"

Okay. That was the absolute *last* thing I expected him to say. "Really? You want to talk about this now?"

While you're in your underwear?

I don't say that part out loud. I don't have to. Max understands, and he stalks a little closer to me.

Taking the bundle of clothes in my hands from me, he adds it to the pile of his, then sets it by the back door, as far from me as it can get while we're both still in the kitchen.

"The wolfsbane is wearing off now that we've gotten rid of our clothes. It'll take time to wash them, and it's just a little nudity between... friends." The way he tastes the word as he says it tells me that Max isn't so sure that's the one that fits... but what else can it be? "I don't want to think about the wolfsbane. Not now. Not while I can't do anything about it until tomorrow. But you're here, and I'm here, and I haven't been able to stop thinking about the cupcake you said you made for me since I knew it was supposed to be mine."

I gulp. "It was a caramel apple cupcake."

"My favorite," he grates out.

That causes my cheeks to go pink. "I didn't know. I guessed... but I mean it. I did make it for you. He was supposed to give it to you... I don't know why he didn't—"

"You were trying to feed me."

My mouth falls open. Technically, he's not wrong. I was. Knowing full well the ramifications of what my 'peace offering' could mean, I tried to feed him. "Yes."

"Will you feed me now?"

My heart thuds wildly against my chest. Here's hoping his wolf is still dull enough not to notice how my pulse is pounding. "I don't know if that's a good idea."

He prowls closer to me. "Why not? I fed you earlier."

"Because you're the Alpha. You take care of your packmates."

"I don't see you as only a packmate."

My pulse *spikes*. "What do you see me as?"

It's his turn to look stunned. He opens his mouth, pauses, then scowls, rubbing his forehead.

"I should focus on the murder. That's important. The new zoning regulations in September... they were important, too. I'm the Alpha. I'm the sheriff. There's always something that requires my attention. But what about what I want?"

"What... what is it you want?" I ask softly.

His eyes clear as they look at me. "Something sweet."

My tongue darts out, poking at the corner of my

mouth. "I didn't finish cleaning up my remaining stock when you told me to get packed earlier. I think I have pink lemonade cupcakes leftover you can try."

"Pink lemonade. My favorite."

A nervous chuckle escapes me. "Are they all your favorite?"

"If you baked them? Then *yes*."

"Stay here. I'll go get one from the display."

Max doesn't answer me. He just waits for me to start for the swinging door before he follows me into the front of the store. Fair enough. I didn't stay behind when he told me to earlier.

The lights are still off. Moonburrow is quiet and dark; even if there was a nocturnal shifter on the street, they'd have to have their noses pressed to the front window to see that me and Max are standing behind the counter in our underwear.

We're all but invisible, even when Max grabs me by my hips, perching me on the edge of the back counter once I grabbed one of the pink-frosted cupcakes.

I raise my eyebrows at him.

He gives me a wolfish grin. "I do believe I asked if you would feed me."

He's got a point there. With a small smile of my own, I remove the paper liner and hold out the cupcake. The hunger never leaving his gleaming gold eyes, he takes a bite—and he goes still.

Ah, crap. He doesn't like it. I messed it up. Sugar... did I forget sugar? Or—

Almost as though it's ripped from him, Max makes a low, *sinful* sound in the back of his throat before he growls my name softly.

I lean toward him, closing the small gap between us.

His tongue darts out, lapping at the lick of frosting welling in the corner of his mouth.

Heat floods through me as I gulp. "Good?"

Max lifts his head, staring at me in that all-consuming way of the predator.

My breath catches in my throat as his gaze locks on my face.

"*Delicious.*"

His voice is a deep rumble that has me shuddering. And, sure, I'm sitting on my countertop in my underwear, but I'm not cold. The opposite, actually.

When Max Lobo looks at me like that, I'm on fire.

He moves into me before I can breathe, his palm braced on one hip, the other curling under my chin to tilt my face up. For a moment, we just stare at each other, opossum and wolf.

Then he leans in, slow enough that I could stop him.

I don't.

The kiss is careful at first, as if he's afraid to startle me, but the second I sigh against his mouth, his restraint cracks. The world shrinks to heat and heartbeat and magic flowing between us. He tastes like sugar and pine and *want.*

It's dizzying.

I *love* it.

When he finally pulls away, he lifts his hand. His thumb goes to the corner of my mouth, wiping away a smear of frosting he shared with me like it's an excuse to touch me one more time.

"Don't ask me to forget again, Honey." His voice is barely a whisper. "I'll do anything you ask of me, but don't ask that."

"I won't," I promise.

How can I when I couldn't forget the first time he wanted me to?

Max grins. "*Good.*"

Damn it. He's right there. It would be so easy to confess. To tell him that there's a reason why he feels possessive and protective, and why he can't resist the urge to kiss me.

I open my mouth, the words 'I'm your mate' on the tip of my tongue... but what comes out instead is, "I should shower."

He takes a few steps back. "To wash the taste of me off of you?"

His perceived—and not entirely inaccurate—rejection has his words coming out as sharp as a knife.

I shake my head, desperate to blunt the edge.

"Because I think the wolfsbane got in my hair and my neck is beginning to feel numb."

That does the trick.

With a moment's hesitation, Max lifts me up off the counter, holding me close. "Where's the shower?"

I tap his chest. "I can walk up the stairs."

"And I can carry you."

"Max—"

"You're impossible."

"Ah, you love me."

Max jolts, but he doesn't set me down.

Me? I could almost kick myself for such a flippant quip. That's what I do. I'm Honey Morgan. I have a sunny outlook on life, but I'm as hardheaded as a dog with a bone. I rarely think before I speak, and even when I do, half of what I say is a smartass response.

I don't actually think Max loves me.

Oh, no. The bigger problem is that I think that *I* love *Max*.

That realization stuns me silent. I let him carry me the rest of the way up, and when he glances down at me when we reach the top, visibly puzzled, I point in the direction of the bathroom. Just as stubborn, Max finally sets me down on my feet again, but he doesn't leave until he's figured out how to turn my shower on for me.

Declaring the temp to be perfect, he says flatly, "I'll be waiting for you downstairs. I need to get my clothes so we can wash them for tomorrow. After that, I'd appreciate it if I could borrow your shower."

"Of course—"

"Thank you. And then we're going to finish the conversation we started downstairs."

Crud. Here I thought I got away with it, too.

I nod. "Only for a little bit. I'm tired, and we need to get some sleep."

And I only have one bed. Wonderful. Unlike Max's Alpha cabin, I don't have a guest room, but I guess that's a bridge we'll cross when we get to it. Knowing him, he'll insist on sleeping on the kitchen floor to protect me.

He nods, then steps out of the bathroom.

I wait a few seconds before closing the door behind him. I don't bother with a lock. Max is an honorable male. He won't come back in unless I invite him to, and it's not like a simple lock will ever keep an Alpha out if he decides to return on his own.

Stripping quickly, I test the water, impressed that it's just as hot as I like it. I step in, letting the spray wash over me. Specks of grey appear at the bottom of the tub. Remnants of the wolfsbane that managed to hit me. As I grab some shampoo, lathering my hair, I'm already feeling ten times better as I rinse the rest of the wolfsbane off of me.

That lasts for... oh? Ten seconds?

Yeah. That's about right. Ten seconds... that's how

long it takes before I prove that my impression of Max might not be all that correct because he doesn't just come thundering down the hall of my upstairs apartment instead of heading down the stairs to the bakery. Oh no, he throws open the bathroom door, barging in.

I peek my head around the shower curtain, ready to rip him a new one for not sticking to his word, when I see him—and he sees me.

"Why do you smell like my mate, Killer?" His wolfish eyes flash, a heated look so very different from the cold gaze peering into my window earlier tonight. I shiver all the same. "Why do you smell like *mine*?"

Holy shit.

Holy *shit*.

I... wasn't thinking. I'm running on two hours of sleep, I got hit by a blow-back spell, and Max Lobo's kisses scrambled my brain again.

I wasn't thinking, and I hopped in the shower. What else did I do?

I just washed my scent-dampener charm off and, for the first time since I moved to Moonburrow, my fated mate got a full blast of my scent.

Uh-oh.

The shower curtain yanks back. I get one look at Max, and if I could still drop, I'd be dropping fast.

Only I don't. Instead, I stare at him, unsure what to say—or how to apologize. A low, guttural sound rolls from the depths of his chest. A sound so dominant, it's more instinct than speech. I don't faint, but I do freeze, one hand still in my damp hair.

"Max?"

There's no keeping him away from me. I'm hot and I'm wet—and I don't just mean from the shower. My scent perfumes the air; so does his. He breathes in deep, body flexing. The Alpha doesn't shift, but it doesn't matter. His boxer briefs literally tear right off of him only from the way that his body flexes, his wolf rising to the forefront in an effort to get near its mate.

Naked and oh so tempting, he joins me in the shower, tugging the shower curtain closed behind him. He blocks me, as though thinking I'm going to flee. Going to escape.

Nope. I'm doing everything I can *not* to fling myself at him.

I gulp, staying where I am with the exception of lowering my hands.

"What is that scent?" His voice is rough, strained, almost confused. "It's been there, underneath every-thing. Under sugar, under coffee, under whatever charm you've been hiding behind. And you... you've been hiding it, haven't you? That you're my... my..."

He can't say it.

I force myself to. "Mate."

His eyes flash so brightly, I want to wince. Shit. He's pissed. I figured this would happen, but... "I'm sorry. But you weren't supposed to notice."

He laughs once, sharp and disbelieving. "I didn't. Because you've been *muting* yourself."

Truth's out, isn't it?

I nod. "I had to. You're a wolf, Max. And I'm—"

His hand comes up, trembling just slightly, brushing damp strands of hair from my cheek. "Say it."

"—an opossum," I finish, voice thin. "Prey. And I didn't want you to know. I didn't want you to feel obligated, or worse, disgusted if—"

The growl returns, softer this time, a promise instead of a threat.

"Honey." My name is pure possessive on his tongue. How am I only just noticing that *now*? "You've been mine all along, and you didn't tell me."

It's hard to look at him, and not because he's an Alpha. It's because he *is* my mate, and I hurt him. "You would've treated me differently."

"Damn right I would have," he murmurs, voice thick. "I'd have protected you, stayed close, made sure nothing touched you."

"You did," I blurt out. "You've been doing it all along. As if you knew—"

He shakes his head. "I didn't. I always... No. I didn't know. *You* did."

I can't deny that.

"Yes." The word is a whispered admission. "I've known since the first day I caught your scent. The most delicious pine... you were sitting in your cruiser, writing something down. You glanced up, looked at me for a moment, and I knew. But then you looked away and I also knew that you—"

"What? You thought I wouldn't want you?"

"I thought a wolf would never want an opossum. That's how it works. You're a predator. You hunt. I hide."

Steam from the shower curls between us. Max's fingers hover just above my upper arm, close enough that I can sense the tremor in his prolonged restraint.

"You hid your scent for months," he murmurs, voice impossibly low. "You must've thought I'd tear you apart the second I knew who you were to me."

I swallow hard. "Not tear me apart... I always knew you weren't that kind of predator. I believed that Fate wouldn't have led me to you if that was the case. But see me as something fragile because opossum shifters are classified as prey... something to protect. Something weak—"

His jaw flexes. "You think that's all I see when I look at you?"

I shake my head, flinging water drops everywhere. "I think you see everyone that way, Max. It's not a bad thing. You keep us safe. You're an Alpha. That's what you do."

He exhales slowly. "You have no idea how hard it's been, Honey. Wanting to keep you close and not knowing why. Every time you smiled at me, I wanted to —" He cuts himself off, eyes flicking away. "Doesn't matter."

"It does," I whisper, placing one shaky hand on his chest in the space between his pecs. "Tell me."

His gaze snaps back to mine, eyes wilder than I've ever seen from the self-contained sheriff. "You felt like home. Even before I knew what you were or had any thoughts about who you could be. And I told myself that was dangerous."

The confession lodges somewhere between my ribs. "You're scared," I say softly.

The big, bad wolf is *terrified*.

"Of hurting you," he admits. "A predator doesn't know his own strength sometimes. And you're fierce, Killer. You can be feisty. You're still smaller than I am. In your fur..." He looks my naked body up and down, the heat in his expression burning me up more effectively than the shower spray. "... and in your skin."

I slide my palm up his damp skin, curving my fingers around the side of his throat. "You'd never hurt me. I've known that for a while."

He lets out a rough breath that sounds like a laugh. "You're not afraid of me at all, are you?"

"Of course I am," I admit. "You're a wolf, Max. I'm an opossum. We're not supposed to fit, but Fate says we do. I always knew it. I just... when you didn't, I thought it was because your instincts wanted to keep you from recognizing that I was prey."

"My instincts are idiots." His thumb strokes across my knuckles. "It took me long enough. You had your reasons. I can blame the charm all I want for being blind, but I see you now. You're mine, Honey."

My lips quirk into an honest smile. "That's all I've wanted to hear."

He goes still. "You mean it? You want this? You want me?"

"I do. I always have. I just thought you wouldn't want me."

He inches nearer to me, closing the last bit of space between us. "I've wanted you every damn day since you rolled into town. I just didn't understand why it felt like it hurt me to stay away."

His surprisingly earnest words steal my breath for a moment. I hurriedly catch it, then tilt my head up at him, enjoying the way the shower spray has formed slight curls of water-damp hair on his forehead.

He's my mate. I don't want him to *hurt*.

Good thing this prey shifter can do something about that.

"Then stop staying away," I whisper.

That's all the permission he needs.

Max is an Alpha. I've never been able to forget that. His dominance is a big part of who he is, and his type of wolf gives him abilities that I don't have.

One of them? Speed.

He moves so quickly, so decisively, changing our positions so that my back is to the tiled wall, the shower spray falling between us. His body completely consumes mine. He has one paw on my hip, the other is braced by my head, trapping me beneath him. All I breathe in is Max. His scent. His aura. His *everything*. The length of his erection digs into the side of my belly. His chest is heaving, or maybe that's mine. There's barely two inches separating us.

He bows his head, forcing me to make eye contact. The only challenge going on here is Max daring me to deny him, to deny that I feel this bond thrumming between us, this aching need... our mating dance coming two months too late because of magic and my own insecurities and who knows what else... it's late, but it's here, and the only thing that can come between us now is one word.

No.

I could say it. Max could say it.

Neither of us do.

He tilts his forehead down, leaning it against mine, both of us suddenly trembling in a combination of anticipation and desire. "I'll go slow," he murmurs. "If you change your mind—"

"I won't." My voice is steady now. "I want you. Not gentle, not careful... I know who my mate is. I want everything you have to offer."

For a heartbeat, everything stills. Then he kisses me, slowly at first, like he's memorizing the shape of my 'yes', before the urgency takes over and he's just about devouring me.

The bond hums beneath our skin, some higher power—the Luna perhaps—urging us to accept what Fate has given us.

Pulling away, he uses the tip of his claws to trail along the column of my throat. His wolf is making a further appearance, and that actually makes me feel better. My opossum has been on Team Mate Max since the beginning; it was my human brain that got all mixed up. I want Max and his wolf to choose me. It looks like he might.

He sucks in a soft breath. "I've never done this before."

A nervous lump lodges in my throat. I swallow it roughly. "Does it make me sound like a jealous shrew if I tell you that I'm glad? Because the idea of another female getting to touch you like this... having you touch them... it makes me want to claw their imaginary eyes out."

"I'd do worse to your previous lovers, Killer. So, do me a favor... don't tell me about them."

That's easy. "That's okay. I don't have any. I've never done this before, either."

He growls. "You're a virgin?"

Yup. Roxy might've been teasing me, but it was true. Not every shifter waits until they've found their fated mate to, you know, *mate*. Especially spending so much time around humans, it's actually more common for a shifter of my type to fool around and find out what she likes. Wolves... they have this whole 'mating for life' thing hardwired into their brains. I never wanted to assume that Max would be my first and only lover and I'd be his, but, oh, am I glad that we will be.

I grin up at him. "And not just a Virginia opossum."

I don't know what it is I said. I was just trying to make light of the sexually charged moment and Max's softly uttered admission, but it's like I flipped a switch.

"Where? Here? Your bed? Because my wolf is begging me to get you under him, Honey. If you'll let him... if you'll let *me*... I'm taking you as my mate right now."

Let him? That's all I want.

If we were humans, this might seem super sudden. We're not human. We're shifters—with a bit of witch thrown in the mix—and the weirder part is how I managed to hold off on dropping to all fours in front of him, presenting him my ass so he could mount me for as long as I did. Most shifters, once they recognize the gift that is their one true mate, they claim them almost immediately.

Max knows I'm his—and all of my worries, my fears, my inhibitions... they go down the shower drain with the running water.

Where?

Here sounds good to me.

With an inviting grin, I hook my leg around his hip, opening myself completely up to him.

My predator doesn't hesitate. He goes in straight for the kill—or, in this case, he grabs his cock, positions it at my entrance, and starts to push. Even in the haze of his mating dance-induced lust, he remembers that it means something different for a female to be new to mating than it does a male, whether they're prey or predator.

He said he would be careful. That he would take his time. Despite my insistence that I only want *him,* I should've known better. Max has proven again and again that he doesn't want to hurt me, so careful and slow... that's exactly what he does at first. Kissing me at the same time to distract me from any discomfort, he moves slowly yet possessively, feeding every inch of his cock into my waiting, hot and slick pussy, both of us enjoying the sensation of two becoming one.

I'm not afraid. Not of this. Mating is natural, and if he wasn't meant for me in every way, Fate never would've given us to each other. Sure, he's a pretty big male, and I feel like he's stretching parts of me that could easily tear, but I trust Max.

There's some resistance. I sense it. So does Max. He digs his fingers in my hair, prickling my scalp with his claws. At the same time, he nibbles on my bottom lips and *shoves.*

Okay. It hurts. Like, it burns so bad, I grunt into his mouth, but I'm a shifter. I heal pretty damn quickly. The pain is there and gone, and by the time Max is withdrawing from me, prepared to make a second thrust, all that I'm experiencing is pleasure.

It's more than that. As Max claims my mouth with his, my body with his, rocking into me, pinning me to the wall so that I'm right where he wants me—*under him*—the bond I've worked so hard to ignore is blazing like a dark gold thread deep inside of me. It ties me to his male, and though this is only the beginning of forever for us, I hold on tight and enjoy the ride.

AFTER WE GOT DIRTY IN THE SHOWER, MAX TOOK HIS time and care in cleaning me up. His wolf growled under his breath when he saw the trickle of blood mingling with his seed as it streaked down my inner thigh.

Hey. I told him I was a virgin. He knew that, but as though it really hit him in the moment that he claimed me, he dropped reverentially to his knees and licked my thigh clean. Then, as an encore, he decided to find out what my pussy tasted like.

By the time he had me clawing at his shoulders, writhing on his face, I was almost kicking myself for not throwing myself at Max months ago. I assume by our enthusiastic mating, he's at least tabled his hurt at my hiding from him for so long for the moment, but as he cares for me, wrapping me up in a towel, brushing my hair, and laying me out on my bed... I promise myself that I'll do whatever I have to to make it up to him.

Hey. He's mine now. Once our bond is finalized, we'll have *forever*.

Tonight's a different story. It's almost three a.m. And, thanks to the note on the door, I'm not opening the bakery tomorrow. Of course not. The fact that the poison vial had a blow-back spell on it means we definitely have a witch involved. There's a small twenty-witch coven in Moonburrow. It's another lead, and one that Max plans on us following in the morning once he checks in with Riordan.

Us, I notice, as if I couldn't want this male more...

But since going to see the head of the coven at three o'clock in the morning is pushing it even for me, Max insists that we go to sleep. It's weird to have someone in my bed that isn't a ten-pound opossum, but the moment Max spoons me, I have to wonder how I made it twenty-eight years without his body heat warming me up from the inside out.

I snuggle into him and, endorphins fading to dozy bliss, I close my eyes.

CHAPTER 16
PERFECT TIMING

Max's breath is hot on my ear as he murmurs, "How are you feeling, Killer?"

My eyes quirk open. Turning so I can look at him over my shoulder, I ask, "Are you still going to call me that?"

"After how just you wrecked me?" He chuckles, and I preen. Damn. Getting laid looks good on Max. It's like the tension has fled if only for the moment... and, yeah. I did that. "You're getting off lucky. Unless you'd rather I call you 'mate'?"

I blink. Right. He's my mate.

And that means I'm his.

"Killer is fine."

"I thought so." He laughs again, pulling me even closer. "But you are, you know."

Considering my body is well-pleasured and I'd had his dick inside of me, that's kind of what it means. "I know."

"Not just my mate, either. My *fated* mate. The Luna finally told me."

My breath catches in my throat. "She.. she did?"

"Some Alphas get her blessing. If you lead your pack well, she whispers our mate's name in our ear. Last night... in the shower... she whispered yours to me."

"Honey Morgan," I murmur.

"For now. You'll be Honey Lobo come the full moon."

That's right. I knew that. Both of those things, actually. The Luna helps her Alphas find their mates because she wants her wolf shifters to mate and procreate and add to her worshippers. However, because a pack Alpha taking a mate affects all the shifters under him, it's not as simple as mating and marking. There's a whole Claiming Ceremony, and it only can take place on the night of the full moon.

"So you have until the full moon to change your mind?" I ask into the quiet bedroom.

"Look at me, Honey."

It's an order. Max has been very careful not to tell me what to do—and letting me off the hook when he does and I totally disobey—but there's something about the way he says that.

It's not an order.

It's a plea.

I roll over. Instead of being the little spoon, I'm face to face with a predator—and there isn't anywhere I'd rather be.

He wraps one arm around me. With his other hand, he tips my chin up so that I have nowhere to look but at his gleaming gold shifter eyes.

"I'm not changing my mind." His eyes shadow over. "Unless you want to change yours."

Me?

I literally just welcomed him into my body. He's been in my heart for a while now. He's been in my head since the first time I caught his scent.

I don't know who I was fooling. Fake it 'til you mate it, right? Well, I fucking faked it, but from the moment Max growled 'mine'… I was his.

I shake my head.

"Good. I'm a fair male. I do my best to lead, and I will lay down my life for my pack. There isn't anything

I won't do for Moonburrow… but if you asked me to let you go? I don't know if I can."

I shrug, snuggling close to Max again. "That's an easy enough solution. I won't ask you."

"So you'll just run—"

Ah, jeez. Who ever heard of an insecure predator? "No, you goof. I have a good life in Moonburrow. My bakery is a success and Gus is happy here, and, well, *you're* here. Why would I run anywhere?"

Max holds me close, quiet for so long that I think it finally got through to him that I'm not going anywhere, that it's safe for him to finally let down his guard long enough that he can sleep.

And that's when he says, "Does that mean I have an adopted opossum son now?"

I burst out laughing. "Well, I am Gus's mom, aren't I?"

"And my mate."

Yes. And his mate.

I take Max's hand in mine, twining our fingers together, ready to kiss his knuckle when something catches my attention.

"What's this?"

It's a small white scar on his first knuckle.

Shifters don't scar. It's one perk of our type of supe. We have rapid generation which means that—unless silver is involved—we can heal any injury except decapitation without a single clue left behind to show that we were hurt at all.

There are only two exceptions, and it's really only one if you think about it. Shifters have to *choose* to keep a mark on their body. Usually that's the mating mark that comes when a shifter either bites or claws their mate, claiming them as theirs. And then there are some shifters... and it's almost always the predators... they choose to leave a scar as a sign of some meaningful battle or challenge.

What's this one? And why haven't I noticed it before?

"Let's call it a reminder."

I'm just about to ask what that means when my mate stiffens.

"Someone's coming," Max announces.

And, yet, he makes no move to untangle his body from mine. Either he's so confident that he can take our unexpected guest effortlessly while butt-naked or he is simply pleased to show off his new mate to whoever is so rudely interrupting our afterglow.

"It's not Gus. He's still back at the cabin. Even if he were here, it couldn't be him. He might be getting a little chunky lately from all of his treats, but he wouldn't make the stairs creak."

As though the person approaching heard my comment, they stomp the rest of the way up the stairs.

That should've been my first clue. My second should've been the way that Max's nose wrinkles a little, muttering, "Trash," under his breath.

I scent it, too. Obviously not as clearly as my wolf shifter mate does, but when my visitor comes wearing eau du dumpster, it's kind of hard to miss.

Plus, there's the fact that they're comfortable walking onto my territory at three a.m. There's only one soul in Moonburrow who would do that, and she's pretty good at picking a lock.

Two seconds later, my suspicions are confirmed when Roxy Kane pokes her head in my bedroom while saying, "Honey, I was gonna leave this downstairs for you, but then I thought I heard something and—*oh*." She blinks, a small smile curving her lips. "Oh. Look at that. My raccoon said... yeah. I still wasn't expecting you up here, handso— Max." Roxy is a lot of things, but she's not the sort of shifter who will make a play for a mated male. Childhood crushes are one thing. Finding me in bed with Max? Yeah. She knows better than to see how fiercely protective a jealous opossum can be. "At least, not until Honey stopped pretending to be things she wasn't. I take it this is a good thing?"

Max growls softly. I smack his chest. "Yes," I tell her simply. "He's my mate."

"Congrats. That actually saves us all some time and trouble." Roxy lifts up her hand, showing off a rolled-up piece of paper about twelve inches long. "Sheriff will probably want to see this, too."

Uh-oh. "Roxy, what did you do?"

She shrugs. "I decided to be Nancy Drew." She waggles the scroll-looking thing. "And I hit pay dirt."

Max sits up, careful to keep as much of his skin covered with the blanket. Smart male. He doesn't want to trigger his mate's jealous side, either. "Let me see."

She starts to cross the room.

I hiss, then cover my mouth with my hand.

Roxy rolls her eyes. "Take a chill pill, Hon. I don't want your predator."

"Sorry," I mumble.

"Nah. It's cool. You only just mated so you'll be super jealous for a bit. I get it. But we still have a couple of murders in Moonburrow to take care of. Lucky for you, I think I figured it out."

What? "You did?"

"See, it was Abigail's death that clued me in. I liked her. Skittish, but nice. So I decided to take a look into it myself. Her office was on the same street as the apothecary. She was going on secret dates with a wolf shifter. I talked to a couple of pals I have"—pals? Roxy has pals? And I shouldn't say that out loud, right? —"and they gave me a name. Turns out he's been spending a lot of time near Witches 'n' Things, too. He claimed he was just doing his job, but check this out. I think he's full of it."

Keeping enough distance between her and the bed, she starts to toss the paper to Max.

Starts to, then pauses. "You sure? You might not like what you see."

"Does this implicate Honey?" Max asks.

"What? No. It's a dude. One of your dudes."

"Riordan?"

"The cursed Beta? Your brother? If he ever lets himself off the chain, he won't poison shifters in the dark, Sheriff. He'll bulldoze the entire damn town."

Hang on—

I look over at my mate. "Riordan is cursed?"

Max's expression is instantly full of guilt. Huh. Looks like we both have secrets... "I can explain later. But you, Roxy... you can explain now. How do you know that?"

An impish shrug. "Let's just say that I don't only deal in oddities and antiques at my store. I'm nosy. I like information. And when my sources tell me that the new witchy baker in town is on the chopping block, I'm going to get all the information I need to take them down." Her yellow eyes gleam in the darkness of my bedroom. "No one messes with Honey but me."

I'm touched. "Thanks, Roxy."

"Don't mention it. And to make it easier, I'll tell you what this is. It's an order form I found. Don't ask me how. Don't ask me where. It doesn't matter. What does is that it ties Talia Winters to one of your wolves when it comes to a mass order of wolfsbane, silver, and nightroot powder… plus a witch fee for unlimited spells."

"Who is Talia Winters?" I ask.

"She's a witch." Duh. "She also owns the apothecary."

And she's been selling wolfsbane, powdered silver, and nightroot powder to a wolf shifter.

Roxy tosses the scroll. Max doesn't open it. Not yet.

All he says is, "Who's the wolf, Roxy?"

"Leo Holloway."

Max snarls, and I just blink in surprise.

Leo Holloway.

Leo, the wolf who was in the bakery when I accidentally gave away the Can't Resist Cupcakes. Leo, who works in law enforcement with Max and would've been at the pack meet where Declan brought my treats —and Max's cupcake. Leo, the glorified meter-maid who was having a discussion with a witch about Abigail's death when Roxy pushed her way into the conversation.

A witch…

How much do I want to bet that that was Talia Winters?

If he had a witch working with him, that would explain the blow-back spell. That's strong witch magic, and she's sold her services—and the poison ingredients—to one of Max's high-ranked wolves.

But why?

All along, he thought I was the target. Same thing happened last night when the wolfsbane blew back on us. But when you think about the cupcake... what if it *is* Max?

I don't know, but I'm all the more determined to end this. I'm sure Max is, too, though he hasn't taken his Alpha stare off of Roxy just yet.

"Where did you get this?"

"Oh, Max... don't ask questions you don't want the answer to."

Welp. Considering Roxy is dressed all in black, with a black beanie covering her hair, and it's three o'clock in the morning... it's probably a good idea to drop that line of questioning.

Especially when she says, "And that's not what you should be asking."

Max scowls. "Then what should I be asking?"

Roxy jerks her chin at the scroll. "What you're going to do about it."

———

Roxy did her part. She gave Max the scroll, winked at me, joked that we should crack a window, then headed out of the bedroom, calling out, "You have fun up there, kids. I'll lock up behind me."

There's no sleeping for Max and me after that.

Luckily, we're supes. Going without sleep isn't fun—I'm totally jealous of Gus right now because he's snoring away on a big queen-sized bed at the Alpha cabin—but as long as we get some food in us, we'll be fine.

While Max looks over the scroll again, I climb out of the bed. Just like how he could sense Roxy before I did, he knows before I even had one foot on the floor that I was moving. He grabs my wrist, tethering me to him.

There's a question in his gaze, and a powerful male bracing for rejection in the way his jaw clenches.

I smile at him. "I'm going to start laundry and cook some breakfast.

The tiniest flash of relief softens his rugged features. "You're feeding me again."

I lean over him, kissing him softly. "Hey. You mated me. You're stuck with me. I might as well give you a reason to want to stick around, too."

Max trails his fingertips over my pulse point. "Hurry back to me, Honey."

Not 'Killer', I notice. That might be the nickname my mate chose to give me, but on the heels of learning that one of the members of his inner circle is a killer... yeah. It's still a thrill to hear his deep, intoxicating voice say my name.

I promise I would, then do everything else I said. There's no doubt in my mind that Max will want to do something about this right away. So what if it's now three-thirty in the morning? We'd had a plan to go to the museum where the witch coven congregates. Now it's all about figuring out a way to get to Talia Winters and Leo Holloway before they hurt anyone else.

After I double-check that the front and back doors are locked—and that Roxy has vanished—I grab our clothes carefully, bringing them back upstairs. I start the washer. Some coffee, bacon, eggs, and toast will be enough to help me feel more, well, alive. Remembering that I have an Alpha wolf shifter in my bedroom, I triple the portions.

Once it's done, I return to the bedroom. By then it's a quarter after four. Max is sprawled on his back, staring up at the ceiling, though he does sit up as I walk in carrying our breakfast.

"I called my brother. I woke him up and told him to head to the Alpha cabin. He'll check on Gus and meet us there around nine. He's my Beta. He needs to know about Leo, but that's one conversation I want to have face-to-face. There's something else I want to talk to him about, too. After that, we'll go hunting for Leo and his witch."

I get that. But...

"Nine? I know we have to eat, and I just switched the laundry from the washer to the dryer so that will take some time... but what will we do until we leave?"

Max smiles. It isn't a full smile, and I can see the

weight of what it means to be both the Alpha and the sheriff behind it, but it's enough.

"Whatever we want."

I KNOW WE HAVE A MURDERER TO CATCH, BUT EATING breakfast in bed with my mate almost made everything we went through last night worth it. It's Max's turn to feed me. He holds the bacon out, refusing to put it down until I nibble on it. I find out he takes his coffee black—which I figured—and he teases me when he sees mine is dark, too, only it reeks of sugar.

What can I say? I have a bit of a sweet tooth, too.

Just like I thought, we don't sleep. Not really. We sprawl out together, my head on Max's chest. I get to doze off, listening to his heartbeat. When I point out he's being quiet, he says he's thinking, and I leave it at that.

Around eight o'clock, he sighs. "We should probably head back to the cabin."

He's right. I'm not happy to climb up and off of him, but he's right. I go and retrieve our clothes from the dryer. This time, he has to go commando; obviously, I don't have a spare change of underwear for him after his... um... loss of control last night meant he exploded his off of him. I put on a fresh pair of panties and a new bra, vividly aware that Max is watching every move I make.

When he notices that I've caught him staring, he grins, showing me the points of his wolf's fangs. Still perched on the edge of my bed, fully dressed now, he pats his lap. I finish buttoning up my jeans and walk over to him.

He shoots his hand out, fingering one of my loose curls.

After our shower, I didn't get to do anything more to my hair than let Max brush it out for me. Normally, I dry my hair, then braid it into two braids that usually rest over the fronts of my shoulders. This is the first time Max has seen me with all my hair down.

"It's pretty," he rumbles.

"You like it like this?"

He shrugs. "I like your hair no matter how you wear it. But the braids... that just makes me think of you."

I'm glad. He's my mate, and my inner opossum's instincts will insist I do anything to keep him happy, but I'm me, too. I'm Honey Morgan. I wear my hair in braids, and as I smile down at Max, I divide my hair in half. With practiced fingers, I quickly do my hair the way *I* like it.

Max gets up. Bending his head, he drops a kiss to the corner of my mouth. "That's my mate."

A shiver courses down my spine. It's only been a

few hours, but I swear: I'll never get tired of hearing him say that.

We leave shortly after that. I completely forgot that Max parked in front of the bakery. At the time, I didn't think we'd end up spending the night. Now? Anyone who got up early and traveled down Sycamore Street knows that the sheriff kept his car here overnight.

Shifters gossip worse than little old ladies. Possessive predators can be just as bad. I wouldn't be surprised if, by the end of today, all of Moonburrow knows that Max and I are mates. His wolf will want to show me off, and I look forward to it... as long as we can close this case first.

I feel a pang when we leave through the front door, locking Dough You Believe in Magic up behind us. This is the time of day that I should be getting my first customers. I even see Betsy hopping down the street toward me, as though this is her destination. It's possible. I'd expected her to come by yesterday when the news about Abigail broke, but they seemed to be friends. Maybe she didn't know yet. Maybe she did, but she was grieving and didn't need an eclair.

She waves at me, hurrying up. Normally, I'd make small talk. But, normally, I'm not worried about going after a wolf and a witch. Since Betsy is neither, I wave back before reaching for the passenger side door.

It's okay. I'll make it up to her at the next prey circle

meeting. Who knows? Maybe I'll even provide the snacks next time.

I reach for the passenger side door—but Max is already there, holding it open for me.

I flash him a grin as I sink into the seat. My chivalric mate nods, closing the door for me, before prowling around the front of the car to get to the driver side.

CHAPTER 17
RIORDAN

Twenty minutes later, Max is pulling up to the Alpha cabin. Because I can sense he needs to do this, I wait until he opens the door for me. A sliver of relief coupled with affection flitters down the fledgling tie that bloomed into being as soon as we admitted we were mates.

It's so easy to look at the Alpha not knowing that I was *his* and blame the scent-dampener charm. I'm no angel. I did that on purpose, applying it like perfume everyday religiously. I was a coward. Prey shifter, yeah? I was afraid that he would reject me so I didn't give him the chance.

But there's something more to it. He's an *Alpha*. Maybe when I was just another prey shifter in Moonburrow, it was easier to overlook me while I was wearing the charm and running a charmed bakery. As soon as we started spending time together, though, it should've been obvious… and, in a way, it was. We went from being strangers to mates in less than a week, with him kissing me long before I washed off the scent-dampener.

Something was messing with Max. I didn't know what, but I'd figure that out, too. If only for his peace of mind and mine, I would.

First, though, we needed to fill Riordan in on what happened.

Max opens the door to the Alpha cabin, stepping aside to let me in. Good thing, too, since a ten-pound white-and-grey torpedo comes bounding at me the moment I walk inside. Gus does figure eights around my sneakers, chittering the whole while, swishing his tail as though scolding me for staying out all night with my new boyfriend.

No. Not my boyfriend.

My *mate*.

I laugh in delight. Bending low, I scoop up Gus,

hugging him to my chest. I know that Max said that he was sending Riordan to keep Gus safe. That warmed my heart more than I can say, and I'm so glad to see that Gus is alright.

Following Max's lead, I carry Gus into the living room. I remember walking by it yesterday to get to the guest room. Today, we go in as a trio.

Riordan is waiting for us there. There is a love seat on one side of a squat coffee table. To its left, and up against a window, there's a sofa. Riordan is leaning back in the love seat, one arm stretched along the back, his ankle resting casually on his knee.

Max nods at him. I give him a small wave.

He breathes in deep, eyes going wide as he realizes that we're wearing each others' scent.

Unfolding his legs, he starts to rise. "Luna damn it. When you didn't come home, I was worried, little bro, but I guess I shouldn't have been. Congratulations—"

Max shakes his head. "I appreciate it, and I can't wait to introduce Honey to you and Mom and Dad as my mate"—um, *what*?—"but that's not why I told you to meet me here." He had stuck the scroll in his back pocket when we got out of the car. Taking it out, he tosses it to his brother. "This is."

It takes Riordan less than a minute to make sense of the document signed by Talia and Leo, detailing the contract of services and the orders he placed through her. Just like me, Max, and Roxy, he instantly agrees that this is a smoking gun. At the very least, Leo is up to his fuzzy ears in the creation of the shifter poison. Add in Abigail's unfortunate murder and it becomes clear to all of us that he definitely played a part.

Only one problem.

Riordan lowers himself to the love seat. Me and Max are sitting together on the sofa, Gus curled up on my lap. As though he can sense the other wolf needs him, Gus scampers from my lap to the coffee table, rising up on the edge so that Riordan can give him scratchies.

Tossing the scroll away from him, the Beta absently scratches the underside of Gus's chin. "We don't have proof. Proof that he was in on the poison deal, maybe. But we want to get him for murder, don't we?"

Obviously. This is a shifter town, though. Do we really need *proof*?

Actually, I know the answer to that. We do. Of course we do. If Max just took out packmates all willy nilly, who would trust him to lead? He'd be a murderous dictator, not an Alpha.

My mate knows it, too.

"He's working with a witch. We can get the coven involved, but they'll side with one of their own without proof. All we have is a contract, and since Roxy will be a target when it gets out that she gave it to me, I can't use it."

I squeeze his thigh, grateful that he's protecting my friend. "We'll figure something out."

Riordan clears his throat. "I might have an idea." All eyes on him as Gus settles down to curl up on the coffee table near him, he adds, "He seems to be targeting Honey for some reason. I say we let him."

Excuse me? "You want him to kill me?"

"Of course not. That's ridiculous. We just let him think that he *can* kill you."

Max growls. I don't even attempt to stop him. Like, really? What the hell, Riordan? I thought you were cool.

"Let me explain. She's an opossum, yeah? We know she has that fancy trick where she plays dead. We can do this two ways. Either she goes catatonic, letting Leo think someone beat him to it and she's safe because he thinks she's dead, or we let him try to hunt her down and, when he tries, she faints, and we let him think he scared her to death. Either way, he might target someone who is already 'dead', and we can use her as a third victim to get proof without her having to die."

"But what if he *does* kill me? For, like, realsies?"

"He won't. We'll be there. We'll be the witnesses. And then we'll make him talk."

Max was silent during the outlining of Riordan's plan. You'd think he was just dismissing it as a poor one. Nope, he was trying to keep his temper in check before he completely exploded.

Oh, like he does *now*.

"Have you lost your mind? You want my mate to be bait? Right after I found her?"

I stroke the side of his neck, trying my best to calm him. "Technically, *I* found *you*."

"You did, and then you hid in plain sight for months. Now my eyes are wide open. Declan was one of mine. So was Abigail. Leo was in my inner circle, but I didn't see the danger lurking there, either. I do now. I can't let you do this."

"Can't?" I ask. "Or won't."

And that's the thing about mating a predator. They will always, always outrank you when it counts. They're stronger, faster, more fierce. I act like I can ignore any of his commands, but if Max really put his wolf into it, I'd be unable to do anything but bare my throat and submit to him.

That's not how it works for mates. If there's any imbalance in the mating at all, it's the more dominant partner bending over to raise up their weaker mate.

If I want to go along with Riordan's cockamamie plan, I should get to choose. If Max can make this decision for me without any pushback, what happens the next time he thinks he knows better?

We're not bonded yet. Oh, we have a bond. I can't pretend that doesn't exist. It did even before the physical act of sex. But now that we *did* mate, if we perform the shifter Claiming Ceremony, I'll be tied to Max Lobo for the rest of my life. Not yet, though.

Not *ever* if this doesn't work...

"It has to be Honey," Rirodan says softly. "I'm sorry, but you know I'm right. Whoever is hurting our pack-mates, they've gone after her. The cupcake... the tea... they involved her in this. But we have the element of surprise on our side. Most of Moonburrow still thinks she's a witch. Not everyone knows that she's an opossum shifter. He won't think she's playing dead. He'll think she *is* dead. Remember? Even we were almost fooled."

That's right. I didn't wake up in the morgue, but it was a close call the way they were peering down at me in the alley behind the bakery. They thought I was almost dead until I wasn't.

But if Riordan's whole insane plan hinges on me being able to play possum... we might have a small problem.

"Yeah. One thing about that... I don't think I can play dead anymore."

"What?"

That's both of the Lobo brothers at the same time. I shrug, trying to appear way more casual than I feel.

"It's something I noticed after I found Declan. I dropped like I normally did, but when I woke up, Max was there. The next time I thought I was going to faint, he steadied me. Anytime I've felt weak, he was right there to give me his strength. My opossum," I say, tapping my chest, "can sense his wolf. She knows that Max... all of Max... will protect us. I don't need to faint anymore because there's nothing that he can't protect me from."

Max loops his arm over my shoulder, tugging me to him so that he can kiss the top of my head before tucking me against his side. He doesn't say anything. He doesn't have to.

His promise to keep me alive is thrumming down our bond.

But Riordan just won't let it go.

"I can help with that."

Max sits up, moving so quickly that I nearly land on my side behind him when I fall over. "Riordan—"

"No, Max. It's okay. You mated her and that makes her family. She ought to know."

It takes me a second to push myself back to a seated position. Max, looking abashed, helps, but I brush him off. Oh, no. I'm way more interested in what his brother just said.

Know why? I think I might have a clue. Score one for Miss Marple. "Roxy said you were cursed."

That takes the wind out of Riordan's sails. His head shoots right toward his brother.

Max holds up his hands, leaning back into the sofa. "I didn't tell her."

Riordan frowns. "No one else knows."

"Trust me, that doesn't mean anything when it comes to Roxy." Case in point, the scroll on the coffee table next to Gus. "So what does this curse mean? And why do you think you can help me? Do you, like, turn into a scary beast or something?"

Riordan gives me a droll look. "I'm a big, black wolf half the time. Isn't that scary enough?"

Maybe before I mated a predator. "No."

"Well. That's not it anyway. It's worse." He exhales. "A lot worse."

"Come on. It can't be that bad."

"Fine. But don't say I didn't warn you. About fifteen years ago, when Max and me were in our teens... he was sixteen and I was nineteen... I knew that I was the Alpha-heir. When Dad stepped down, I would take over the pack. I didn't earn it. I didn't challenge him for it. It was going to be handed to me, and I was a cocky prick about it."

"Riordan..."

"It's okay, bro. I know it. I treated everyone in Moonburrow like shit. I treated you like shit because you would be my Beta." A hollow laugh escapes him. "I thought I was untouchable... until I angered a witch who was passing through. I told her to get out of Moonburrow if she wasn't going to respect me. She said I needed to learn to earn it. I told her that I would one day be Alpha and everyone would listen to me.

"She said, 'Why wait?,' and she cursed me so that,

any order that comes out of my mouth, whoever hears me has to listen. They *have* to listen. They *have* to obey. It's what I thought I wanted, but the reality is... how can you lead if you steal your pack's free will? Who would follow me?"

I know the answer to that: *no one.*

A lot of things suddenly make sense. How Riordan is so careful to say things like 'should' and 'suggest'. He gives options and opinions, and all along, I thought it was because he didn't want to step on the Alpha's toes.

Oh, no. He must've stepped down, letting Max become the Alpha instead, the older brother relegated to the Beta role he once scorned.

Huh. No wonder his laugh was so hollow...

"Damn," I say. And that's all I said.

"It sucks," he agrees, the understatement of the year. "But I've learned control. An Alpha doesn't demand obedience. He commands loyalty. I've strived to do that. Max is our Alpha. My job as his Beta is to support him. In this case, he's too close to you. He won't want to risk you."

He's right. Max wouldn't.

But what if I wanted to help? That's what my attempt at amateur sleuthing was all about, after all. What began as wanting to clear my name—and my bakery's rep—turned into something more.

This is Max's pack. His *life.*

"How would it work?"

"Honey—"

"You wear an ear plug," Riordan says, conveniently ignoring the fact that Max spoke up at all. I guess, on Max's territory, his older brother has the leniency to be the true alpha he was born to be. "A wire. You give me the signal if you see Leo. Over the line, I'll tell you what to do. If I command you to 'play dead', you will. Max will be right there. As soon as we have Leo in custody, I'll bring you back. There's no danger involved."

"Then why don't you ask *your* mate to do it?"

Riordan grimaces, and Max runs his hand over his face.

"Fuck. I'm sorry. I shouldn't have said that. It's just… I can't lose her. When you find your mate, you'll understand."

A small, humorless smile tugs on Riordan's lips. "When I find my mate, my curse will be broken and I wouldn't be able to do this in the first place. But I can. It'll be safe, Max. I understand if you want to come up with another plan. That's fine. Either way, we have to get Leo. If he's plotting behind your back and has enough help that we've been in the dark all along, he's too dangerous to be free."

"He doesn't know we're onto him. There's time."

No. There isn't. I lift my hand. "Screw it. I'll do it."

"Honey—"

Sorry, Max.

"I'll do it, but on one condition." Turning in my seat, I focus on Riordan. "I want to know if you ever used your curse on Max. And I don't mean something silly." Suspicion sparked the instant Riordan confessed what exactly his curse entailed. Maybe I'm wrong... but I have to ask. "Did you do something that would keep him from recognizing that I was his fated mate?"

Max sucks in a breath. I get it. I'm basically accusing his brother of taking his free will away from him right after he made a speech about how he changed. It's messed up, but what if he *did*?

"What? Of course not! I would never—" He stops suddenly, his tanned skin paling. "Shit."

"Riordan?"

He gets up. Every time I've ever seen Riordan Lobo, he's been immaculate. Clothes stylish and pressed, not a single hair out of place.

Until now.

He runs his fingers through his hair, pacing back and forth in front of the coffee table. From his place on top of it, Gus mimics his movements, keeping company with the Beta.

"Shit. Max... let me say this first: I didn't do it on purpose. I swear it to the Luna. If I did... it was completely on accident."

Max digs his fingers into the couch. Hopefully they're not claws otherwise he's going to have a whole bunch of slash marks in the leather. "What did you do?"

"Remember back in September when we were dealing with the zoning laws? We had that lawyer stop by the station with the papers."

Max's face shadows over. "Abigail. I remember." His gaze darkens. "It was all about redrawing the unofficial borders of Moonburrow. The witches wanted more land. The predators refused to concede. The prey shifters were staying out of it. It was giving me a headache and I told Abigail to discuss the papers with Leo."

Well. At least we know when they could have met...

"Right. You went out for a drive, and when you came back, you told me that Jean Douce's granddaughter had arrived to take over the bakery. You said she smelled like caramel and something that was making your wolf go wild." Riordan gives me an apologetic look. "You wanted to go back and talk to her. I... I snapped at you to focus. That the zoning shit was important. We got it done, but you never went back to the bakery."

Not until the fiasco with the Can't Resist Cupcakes meant that I had a couple of complaints that brought the sheriff to my door...

Max stares at Riordan. "I remember that. Everything else seemed so important, but every time I smelled caramel, it was like I was missing something."

I bump my shoulder against his. "You were. *Me.*"

Max shifts so that he's facing me. "And you're asking me to put you in danger?"

"No." I pat my mate on his handsome cheek. "I'm asking you to let me help you close this case so that we can put all these murders behind us. Besides, I trust you. You won't let me die."

He won't, and I believe that with every last inch of my soul.

"Declan needs justice. No matter why Leo went after him, he needs justice. So does Abigail." Her sad eyes flicker through my mind. "I don't want him to hurt anyone else. Not me." I stroke the edge of his jaw. "Not you, either."

Put like that, how can he refuse?

Spoiler alert: he can't—and he doesn't.

Riordan had a good plan. It hinged on both him and Max dousing themselves in wolfsbane. Gus was brought to their parents' cabin at the other end of the woods—I stayed back because I absolutely refused to meet Max's mom on a couple of hours of sleep—so that he was protected. Riordan handpicked a few wolves that were one hundred percent loyal to Max in case we needed backup.

Do I know where he got the ear thingy and the wire from? No. Do I ask? Also no. I figure, these two aren't just the Alpha and the Beta of the pack that is responsible for me and the town. They're the top law enforcement officials in Moonburrow. I guess this goes with it.

It was a sting; look at me, using detective lingo. I was bait, and I did a good job. Figuring that it was Leo that Gus saw peeking at me last night, if he was still coming after me, he'd be watching the cabin. Max confirmed that Leo had an apartment downtown, but Declan was an old friend of his. He would sometimes stay over at his cabin if pack meets ran late.

It's another reason why neither Max or Riodan ever thought it could be Leo. Declan was his friend. Abigail was his... something. He worked closely with Max... but it didn't matter. He was involved, and we needed to prove it for the sake of Moonburrow.

That was actually way easier than I thought it would be. I stayed inside the Alpha cabin with Max while Riordan made his plans; another way that my mate let his brother use some of his obvious alpha energy. A little before sunset—since I didn't want to get caught in the dark, just in case—I announced enthusiastically that I would be taking a walk.

Right on time, one of their loyal wolves came knocking at the door. Riordan sent Vera, a maternal delta who looked like she couldn't hurt a fly... unless her pups were in danger, that is... to ask the Alpha for a meeting in the den. This was all pre-arranged, of course. If Leo was watching and saw that Vera and Max were going in one distraction, Max's new witchy pet going wandering off into the woods again at the same time, Riordan thought he might not be able to resist coming after me.

He was right.

I hadn't even made it as far into the woods as we went last night before a very familiar, and scarily friendly face popped out from behind one of the taller trees. If I was clueless, I'd think he was just another wolf in Moonburrow looking out for one of the weaker residents.

I knew better.

It was the eyes. It's always the eyes. Sure, his smile was odd, his mouth crowded with teeth, but there was an unwell, *hungry* gleam in his eyes that told me that this was no normal predator.

This was someone on the wrong side of being feral.

It happens. When you're part human, part beast, sometimes a shifter goes bad. You start thinking that you can live outside of the pack rules, but instead of going lone wolf, you *break*.

Somewhere along the lines, that happened to Leo Holloway. If I had any doubts that he was a killer, they're squashed the moment I see his eyes. I didn't even listen to the kind greeting or the way he asked if I knew where Max was. I just ran.

He bolted after me.

Luckily, I didn't panic. I didn't faint, either, which was good considering our plan, but I did hit the alarm signal that told Riordan I was in trouble. Just like he coached, he ordered, "Play dead," through my earbud —and that's the last thing I remember until I was blinking my eyes open again, the echo of his voice drawling, "Wake up, Honey, wake up now or Max will gut me."

I'm instantly awake.

I've woken up in the morgue. In body bags. Sprawled out on the asphalt, my head tucked in the Alpha's lap. Waking up on the forest floor, a stick jabbing me in the ass... it could've been worse, but when I see Max crouched in front of me, thrumming in place as he waited for me to stir... when I see the look of pure love and relief flashing across his face as he hurries to help me to my feet... hell. I can't complain.

"Where is he?" I ask.

Max moves me so that I can see if Riordan's plan worked.

It *did*.

The big Beta is pinning Leo's arms behind his back. The blond wolf is thrashing, trying to break free of Riordan's hold. Good luck, asshole. He's about twice as wide and an alpha wolf moonlighting as a Beta so, yeah, I don't see that happening.

I think he figures that out at the same time. At the very least, he goes still, but only long enough to throw a hate-filled look at me.

"What are you doing alive? You're supposed to be dead! Even if I failed, it was worth it to see *him* suffer."

Ha! I knew it. I knew that this was all about Max, not me. "Sorry to disappoint. I'm still living." I give him an impish shrug. "Opossum."

His eyes nearly bulge out of his head. "You're another rat? Like that nasty piece of vermin you let into the bakery? I thought you were a witch!"

I am. Part witch on Grandma Jean's side, thank you very much, even if I wish I had more magic than I do because I'd love to zap Leo in the nuts for calling Gus 'vermin'.

He shakes his head wildly. "I should've killed you when I had the chance! Instead of using you to fuck with Max before I stole his pack from him, I should've killed you! He thought you were something. I knew better. You're nothing but worthless prey."

And he spits at me.

Oh, Leo. You shouldn't have done that…

Max gestures for me to take a few steps back. I know better than to even test his patience at the moment. I move, and my mate looks directly at his brother.

"Release him."

What?

Riordan cocks his head. "Yeah?"

"*Yeah.*"

Riordan lets go of Leo, doing what I did and backing

away to give the other two wolves space. Good thing, too, because Max launches himself at the other wolf.

I get it. By threatening me, Leo pushed Max to the point where he had to take the disrespect as a challenge. In a shifter challenge, you fight to either submission or death, and whatever shape you begin the fight in, that's how you better finish it.

I don't know what Leo's wolf looks like. In his skin, he's of a similar height and shape as Max. There's no denying, though, that the Alpha has dominance on his side. While the fight is bloody and brutal, it's also quick. Before I can even work up any concern for my mate, he has Leo pinned under him, body to the dirt.

In one quick motion, Max reaches into his pocket, yanking something out. It's an injection, a shot, and whatever is in the vial, it's thick and silvery. At least, that's all I can see before he jabs it into Leo's neck, thumb pressing on the plunger.

Despite the bloody gashes that Max gave him, it's the shot that has Leo reacting the most like he's been harmed. Bucking his body, he demands, "What the hell did you just do to me?"

"I need answers. You will calm down. You will stop threatening my mate." He takes Leo by the back of his shirt, forcing him to his feet, giving him a small shake as he says 'mate'. "This will help."

"Cheater," Leo snarls. "I could've taken you."

"I was winning our challenge," Max says flatly. "There was no way out of it but death for you. That's too easy. For the sake of the packmates I lost, I will hear your explanation."

"Fuck you!"

"Give it time. The quicksilver should be working its way through you."

Leo goes still. "What do you mean? Quicksilver? What fuck did you do to me?"

That's fear in his voice this time, and I'm glad to hear it. He deserves it.

"Depending on the dose, a shifter can be knocked out or simply cut off from their wolf. But this is a special mixture. Once I knew a predator had to be involved, I went to Delilah." Oh. I know Delilah. She's the head witch in Moonburrow, and a friend of my grandmother's. She also likes jelly donuts. "You see, Leo, you're not the only one who can work with the witches. And yes, I know about Talia. But Delilah... she charmed the quicksilver for me. Until it wears off, you have to answer everything I ask with the truth. And I'll know if you do."

Max glances at me. "I got the idea from the Can't Resist Cupcakes. Let's see if Delilah's charm works as good as yours, Killer."

It must because Leo's face goes motionless for a moment, his eyes glassy, and then he howls. "Those fucking cupcakes! That's what started this whole thing in the first place!"

Huh?

"Do you know how hard I worked, how long I planned to overthrow you? To get the pack on my side so that when I challenged you, there would be no doubt that I deserved to be Alpha? And then I tried one of her cupcakes and I blurted out my whole plan—and she heard me!" Um... no. I didn't. "Of course I had to make her pay!"

Really? That's news to me.

Max, too, it seems.

"But why Honey? Why did you involve *her*? Because you thought she could stop you in your attempts to take over Moonburow?"

Yeah, right. I don't know what Leo is talking about. The honesty cupcakes fiasco had me so focused on cleaning up the mess that I didn't even hear what he was saying that day! I remember a wolf saying something, but compared to Frannie's confession and the fallout from the others, I never knew what Leo said.

"Because I knew she was your mate," he snaps. "You didn't, but I did, and I made sure you stayed away from her... until those Luna-damn cupcakes! You went to her. What happened next? I sent Declan to try to catch her attention... witches don't have fated mates. They can be one, but they don't have one. If he flirted with her... if he made her his mate... you'd lose. Only she didn't even notice. She gave him special food *for you*. She was trying to feed you! And when I told Declan that he needed to throw the cupcake away, he said he couldn't. The damn fool was loyal to the Alpha. He didn't want *me* to be Alpha. I had to kill him!"

Leo laughs. The joyless sound sends shivers down my spine. "I needed a tester for the poison anyway. I convinced Declan that the Alpha was going to meet him at the bakery after the pack meeting. So he could say thank you for the cupcake, and reward Declan for being loyal and leading him to his mate. But I took the cupcake, I poisoned it, and I held him down while I forced him to take a bite. He tried to fight, but a little wolfsbane stopped that. Besides, *I*'m supposed to be the Alpha. Of course I'd win. I hated to kill him, but I had no choice. He wasn't loyal."

Max's jaw goes tight. "And Abigail? Was she loyal?"

Leo barks out a short laugh. "She thought we might be mates. I let her think so. Having a lawyer on my side... she was so damn scared all the time, but I did my best. I asked her to do one thing. Give the witch... the opossum... *whatever*... give her the tea. She did that. I thanked her just the way she liked, but do you know what she did? Made herself a cup! Dumb bitch drank the poison on her own because she felt bad for helping me kill the baker."

Oh, Abigail... I know I should hate her for trying to kill me, but I... I get it. If she believed that Leo was her mate, she would do anything to make him happy. I would do anything—but I'm pretty sure I'd draw the line at murder...

"And last night?" adds Max. "Were you trying to attack my mate on my territory?"

"Would it matter if I said 'no'? I just wanted to look at her. A male can look, can't he?"

Ew. No, thanks. And that, I'm pretty sure, was a lie.

Crap. Maybe Delilah's charm works well, but it's wearing off fast—a fact I'm pretty sure of when Leo turns a hate-filled look on my mate now.

"Hey. I have a question for you, *Sheriff*," Leo says, his voice getting a little more snappish. Damn it. The quicksilver really is wearing off. We won't be able to trust what he says much longer, but that's okay, I guess. We know most of what we needed to know.

We know why Declan died.

We know what happened to Abigail.

So when Leo asks, "How did you know a wolf was involved?," I have to admit that I'd kind of like to know the answer to that myself. Max said he knew... but how?

For a second there, I wasn't sure that Max would answer. Shockingly, he does.

"The peppermint is what really made it obvious. Wolfsbane should've been enough to hide your scent when you were in the alley. But you wanted to make it hurt. Only a wolf knows how bad peppermint extract stings to one of us."

Leo curses under his breath. "I knew I shouldn't have listened to—"

He clamps his mouth shut.

Max shakes him. "Who? Who told you to use peppermint? We know about Talia... who else helped you with this?"

"Wouldn't you like to know?" He spits at Max's feet. Yeah... the quicksilver is totally done now, isn't it? "There are more of us than you know. Stop me. You can't stop us all."

Yeah. We'll see about that.

WE HAVE OUR PROOF. A CONFESSION DOES IT, AND because Leo was feral enough that he did his big villain monologue in front of me, Max, Riordan, and the phone in Riordan's pocket that he set to record as soon as this madness began earlier today, that should be good enough for now.

At least, that's what I thought. Turns out, we aren't quite done yet.

Riordan pulls out another injection, jabbing it into Leo's neck. The second dose of quicksilver is more than enough to put the feral wolf under. He snarls the entire time the sedative does its stuff, eventually spitting and snapping his blunt human teeth before he collapses on the dirt.

Max isn't taking any chances. He zip-ties Leo just in case the quicksilver fails again. It won't trap him permanently, but it should hold a weakened shifter long enough to take him down—and out—again.

Once he's no longer a threat, Max throws back his head and howls.

It's amazing, seeing a wolf's cry pour out of his very human throat. He taps into his wolf to make it, using so much of his power to send the howl out to every pack-mate in hearing distance.

It's instinctive. If I ever needed proof that nothing Max did could ever have me playing dead, that does it. Because I don't. I don't wobble. I don't faint. I just stand in the clearing with him and his brother as dozens and dozens and dozens of wolf shifters come running toward us.

Some of them are in their skin. Some in their fur. From what I can see, they're all mature shifters in the prime of their life; no gammas, no pups.

I don't know who they seem more surprised to see: an opossum shifter standing between the Alpha and the Beta, or the unconscious fair-haired wolf at Max's feet. I'd say it's pretty evenly split, but before I can really get a gauge of what's going on here, Riordan looks at Max, a question in his expression.

Max nods.

Riordan raises his voice. "The wolves of the Moon-shadow Pack have gathered. They've answered their Alpha's call. But we have another who believes he should rule."

Showing off how strong he is, Riordan squats down, careful not to muss his shiny shoes or wrinkle his pants. I can only imagine how much Leo must weigh, unconscious as he is, but Riordan lifts him up easily. He carries him about ten feet away from Max, dropping him back to the dirt before rejoining his brother and me.

"Now... show respect to your Alpha."

It's a command. Just like when Riordan told me to 'play dead', he's used his curse to his advantage. I've experienced the weight of his order. There is no way to refuse.

As one, every single shifter—in their fur, in their skin if they shifted back, or in the clothes they were wearing when they got called out—goes down on one knee.

A majority of the wolves genuflect in the clear direction of Max. But there are some... nine, maybe ten... who turn toward Leo's body as they lower themselves to the dirt.

I gasp.

Max nods at Riordan again.

"If you pledged loyalty to the traitor... if you would

have followed Leo Holloway to the ends of his insanity... stay where you are. Everyone else, rise."

I wince this time. At least three others wolves stay down. It's still a small number. Maybe twelve out of a hundred, but even one betrayal is like a dagger to Max's chest.

Not that you could tell from his flat expression.

"Honey." His voice is gentle, but strong as he addresses me. The sudden wariness trickling down our bond clues me in to how Max is really feeling. "You don't have to be here for this if you don't want to. Riordan can bring you back to the cabin."

"I'd be honored to, Alpha," Riordan calls out, making it absolutely clear where his loyalty lies.

He might have been born to be an Alpha. The curse might have taken it from him. Unlike Leo, he didn't grow feral and twisted with hate. He didn't try to overthrow the Alpha of the Moonshadow Pack without even giving Max the decency of trying to challenge him first.

No. Leo turned to murder while—and maybe I'm biased now—Riordan has become the best damn Beta ever.

He moves near me, keeping his distance because, well, the big male *isn't* my mate.

Max doesn't shift an inch, though I can sense how badly he wants to wrap me up in his arms and hold me close, shielding me from the realities of our supernatural world.

He's a predator. I knew that going into this. As the sheriff, he needed proof that he caught the supe who killed Declan Rowe and was responsible for Abigail Cloverfield's death. As Alpha, he needed to make an example of them so that the pack could have justice.

And he's terrified that I'll see this side of him and suddenly change my mind about being his mate.

Never gonna happen.

I scamper over to him. Going up on my tiptoes, resting my hand possessively on his shoulder, I grab his jaw with the other one. I tug Max toward me and, with all of the packmates gathered acting as witness, I kiss him.

You could hear a pin drop.

I grin against his lips, squeezing his trap as I pull back, dropping to my feet.

"I love you, Max," I tell him, and though the kiss was for the pack's benefit, the words belong to my Alpha. "I'll be waiting for you at the cabin when you're done."

He's a predator, but he's mine, and that's all that matters now.

EPILOGUE

Thanksgiving is a shifter's dream holiday. A day full of food and family, community and gratitude... what can be better?

Oh. I know. A Claiming Ceremony.

Opossum shifters have it easy. When we decide someone is our mate, we mark them, we fuck them, we mate them. Both mates have to go into it choosing each other, but as soon as the claiming is done, a bond snaps into place, and *boom*: we're forever mates.

Wolves are a little more complicated, especially when your mate is the Alpha. First, you need the Luna's blessing. Second, you need to mate on the night that she's full—like tonight. And third, if you're not already marked, you better be by the time you finish.

As Alpha of the Moonshadow Pack, Max hosted a feast for all of Moonburrow. As my mate, he decided that he wouldn't wait until the next time the Luna rose —during the next full moon—to finalize our bond. That's why, once the dessert had been served and the sun had set, our entire community gathered in the woods outside of the Alpha cabin to celebrate the first stages of an Alpha Claiming Ceremony.

Over our heads, the moon above Moonburrow hangs low and full, heavy with a gleaming pale light that spills over the clearing like melted sugar.

The wolves stand in a wide semicircle, their fur silvered, eyes reflecting the glow of their beloved goddess. The prey shifters and witches who join us have gathered along the edge; not out of fear, but respect. Even Gus sits on a stump like a little king, tail curled around his paws, supervising.

At the center of it all, Max takes my hand.

He's not in his version of his sheriff's uniform tonight. No jeans, no badge, just a white t-shirt rolled up at the sleeves, black slacks, and a faint nervous twitch in his jaw that only I can see.

"Ready?" he murmurs.

I nod, even though my stomach is doing somersaults. "You sure you want to tie yourself to an opossum?"

He smiles that slow, dangerous smile that gets me in trouble every time. "You sure you want to spend your life keeping up with a possessive, overprotective wolf?"

"Fair point." I needle him in the side. "Maybe I should change my mind."

Max turns, cupping my jaw in his big paw. "Too late, Killer. I caught you. You're mine. I'm a good male, Honey. A fair sheriff and an understanding Alpha." He banished all of those who followed Leo Holloway out of Moonburrow. Shifter justice was definitely an eye for an eye. Declan died. Abigail. Both Leo and Talia Winters were gone by the time Max finished dishing out supe justice, but everyone else... they got a second chance, thanks to Max. "But if you leave me now, there's no limit to what I'll do to get you back."

I lean into his touch. "As if I'd actually go. Please. In fact, let's hurry this up. I want this bond unbreakable before *you* change your mind."

"Never gonna happen, Honey," he vows, but he does gesture at his brother.

We don't have weddings. It's not a shifter thing. We mate, and we love, and we sometimes have children, but weddings belong to the humans. However, it's a different story when your mate is the Alpha. Their Ceremony is a big deal because it's his way of introducing his mate to the entire pack.

Riordan clears his throat behind us, playing officiant for us.

"Under the Luna's light," he says, voice steady, "we recognize this bond as true and fated. Chosen by instinct, strengthened by choice..."

Max takes my hand, squeezing it. "You sure you're not going to faint?" he whispers.

"I only play dead for dramatic effect," I whisper back. "And not anymore. Not while you're around."

He lifts our conjoined hands, dropping a kiss to the top of mine. "All the more reason for you to accept me as your male."

I snicker. "I thought I did that."

And have done it again and again and, whoops, one more time for good luck in between the salad course and the first round of sides earlier today.

"Choose me, Honey," Max murmurs. "The Luna has already given us her blessing. Choose me."

I look over at Riordan. This isn't a human wedding, but there are no two better words for me to say at this moment than, "I do."

The wolves in the pack howl, a rolling, joyous sound that echoes through the trees and makes every hair on my arms stand up. The prey shifters join in, chittering and squealing and laughing while the witches clap their approval.

Max bends his head close. "Mine," he says quietly, the word more vow than claim.

"Yours," I whisper. "But you're mine, too."

He laughs low in his throat before kissing me under the full moon, surrounded by our pack. His family is here. Mine... isn't. That was on purpose. I love Max and I want to spend the rest of my life with him. Once my mother knows I'm marked and mated and bonded, she'll understand that I was never going to end up with an opossum.

Dad won't care as long as I'm happy.

And Grandma Jean... well, as long as I keep Dough You Believe in Magic running—which I definitely plan on continuing to do like I have been since we solved the murders—she'll be just as tickled as Dad.

For now, though, I need to get to the whole 'marked and mated and bonded' part.

I already have my mating mark. Max couldn't wait. He meant it when he implied that he would never let me go. He's right. He's a good male. If I *really* wanted to leave him, he'd be heartbroken, but he'd let me go if it's what I wanted. The first time we mated, he honestly convinced myself that he would never get the chance to do it again.

Of course, we might be a wolf and an opossum, but we've been going at it like bunnies in the time since we solved the murders. Our second time, Max scraped his fangs over the curve of my shoulder, leaving a pair of thin lines that scabbed over immediately. I kept them, and the look on Max's face when he saw that I *kept* them on purpose... I didn't have to tell him that I chose him and accepted him as my mate. Any time he trails his fingers along the thin white scars, he has all the proof he needs.

Well, except for a finalized bond between us...

Leaving our packmates to celebrate in the woods, Max takes my hand, guiding me back to the Alpha cabin. It's only been a couple of weeks, but in the short time since I've moved here—protective custody becoming *permanent* custody real quick—it's stopped being Max's territory and started to become *ours*.

For the most part, Gus has officially defected to Riordan's side. He sleeps on the Beta's desk in the sheriff's station these days when he isn't coming to the bakery with me, tiny paws resting on Riordan's notebook. Riordan swears he's only keeping him company while I'm working to satisfy all the new customers who want to meet the Alpha's mate, but I'm pretty sure he's been bribing him with watermelon.

It's fine. Max and I have had plenty of other distractions.

Our mating dance was unique. Most shifters recognize their mate and, almost immediately, finalize their bond. Not us. My whole 'fake it 'til you mate it' plan coupled with Riordan's accidental order might've given us a slow start, but we've more than made up for it since then. Nowadays, we're in the early honeymoon phase of a long-lived mating. If Gus prefers to stay with the very single Riordan over listening to me and Max mate most nights, I get it.

Don't blame my little buddy, either.

Ever since the night I claimed Max with my kiss in front of his wolves, we've shared his room. He goes to the sheriff's office every morning unless he's needed in the den; I open the bakery at dawn. But every night, this cabin is ours.

The bakery is mine. The room above it? I've emptied it of everything I brought with me from Glenville. For now, it's just extra space. I'm hoping to hire an assistant at the bakery, maybe offer them the room as part of their salary. If not that, there's always Ashton.

I'm sure my cousin would jump for an excuse to get out of Onancock if Aunt Tessa is treating him anything like my Mom treats me. Who knows? Moonburrow could use another Morgan.

But not tonight.

Tonight is for Max and me, for the night where we pledge ourselves to each other with the Luna our only witness.

And I can't *wait*.

———

MAX STANDS BY THE WINDOW, SHIRT GONE, SLACKS GONE, moonlight sliding over his skin. I look him over, trying to figure out where I'm going to leave my mark on him tonight.

He turns toward me, eyes burning like molten lava. "You ready, Killer?"

The nickname hits softer now. A promise that he'll do whatever he can to see me alive... jeez, I fucking love him.

I move toward the bed. I wore a light pink slip of a dress to our Claiming Ceremony. I'd traded my sweater and jeans and boots for it after dessert because a) it was pretty, and b) I got it for ten bucks. "Almost."

He quirks an eyebrow. "Almost?"

"Sit down, Max."

My powerful Alpha mate has a secret kink. He *loves* it when I tell him what to do in the bedroom. I guess, when he's spent his whole adult life as a dominant wolf shifter, he got used to always being in control. Giving it to me, letting me tell him what to do in the privacy of our mating bed... nothing gets him hotter faster.

In fact, he groans as he sinks down on the bed, beautiful and naked and *mine*.

I don't undress. Not yet. I lower myself between his thighs, stroking his cock absently as I bite the corner of my mouth in deep concentration.

His eyes just about roll to the back of his head. "What... unh... what are you doing? Because I'm primed to explode, Honey, and this is our mating night. I'm not exploding anywhere but inside my mate."

"I know," I say simply, punctuating my statement with a twist of my wrist. He grits his teeth. I grin angelically. "I'm just trying to figure out where I'm going to mark you tonight. Any suggestions?"

"Anywhere," he pants out. "I want all of Moonburrow to know that I'm yours."

Trust me, Max. They already do.

Before I can pick, he lifts up his hand. His hips shift, giving me better access to his erection, though he draws my attention to the small white scar on his finger.

"Remember when I said how this is a reminder?"

It's the bite that Gus gave him. "I do."

"It is. It reminds me how far Gus was willing to go to protect you. You're the most important person in his life. I'm an Alpha, and he bit me for you. If a wild opossum could do that, there's no limits to what I'll do to keep you safe. When you mark me tonight, Killer, I'll have another reminder."

I squeeze him a little tighter. It's only fair, the way

his solemn, grunted words are squeezing my heart right now. "Oh, yeah? And what will that one mean?"

"That I've pledged my life to a wayward opossum with magic. I'll be there to catch her if she drops, and to watch over her if she ever dies on my watch. But only if it's her... what did you call it? A genetic disposition? Because, I promise you this, Honey Lobo, that playing dead is the closest you'll get to the real thing. As long as there is breath in my body, you'll be safe. I won't let you die."

I gasp, releasing Max so suddenly, his cock jerks, searching for the warmth of my hand.

And then, because I'm me, I have one thing to say to that.

"I'm not Honey Lobo," I whisper. "Not yet."

Max reaches out, palming one of my boobs through my dress. "Come here. Once we're bonded, you will be."

I dance out of his reach. "Hang on."

"*Honey...*"

Nope. This is the Alpha's Claiming Ceremony, but this is my mating night, too—and I've been waiting months to make Max Lobo mine.

To make him *ours.*

In a flash, my dress basically exploding off my body, sending pink confetti flying onto the mattress, Max's lap, the floor... in a flash, I shift. My body shrinking, fur bristling, I'm suddenly the small, fierce thing I truly am. My opossum form scurries up his chest until I'm perched right over his heart.

As though he can tell what my intentions are, my Alpha wolf mate tilts his head back. I bite down on his chest.

The moment my fangs pierce skin, an unusual if not unpleasant warmth floods through me. He tastes of blood and hope and tomorrow, and I bite again, creating an image of a heart with my teeth.

Max's breath catches, but he doesn't flinch.

When I shift back, I'm exactly where I want to be: naked and on Max's lap. My hungry mate doesn't even hesitate.

His eyes darken, hunger and awe warring in the same look. "My turn," he murmurs, pulling me closer, shifting me until our groins touch. One quick lift, easy for a shifter as strong as my Alpha, and he seats me on top of his cock.

It's our mating night. The rest is slow and sure. His hands, his mouth, his whispered promises that this is forever, that he loves me, that he'll always protect me...

Ditto, Max. *Ditto.*

The bond finalizes like a rubber band snapping in place between us. Afterward, we stay tangled together as he guides us both backward, my head on his chest, his heartbeat steady beneath the mark I left there.

Outside, the forest is quiet. Peaceful. Our pack is content.

Moonburrow is safe.

No more murders, I think, snuggling up to my bonded mate. No more poison.

No more betrayal, secrets, or lies.

Just a happily ever after, some sweet treats, and a wily opossum named Gus.

What could be better?

BREAD

AUTHOR'S NOTE

Thank you for reading *Fake It 'Til You Mate It*!

This book was such a labor of love for me. I've been writing shifters in this overarching world for nearly five years now, and though I started with wolves in *Never His Mate*, as the world has grown, I added vampires and witches, then finally the concept of sanctuaries and prey shifters.

Honey as an opossum shifter heroine wouldn't exist if it wasn't for a neonatal kitten/wildlife rehabber that I found one day on TikTok. I've always loved opossums and raccoons, but Carley Self (of NOLA Kitten Nursery) taught me so much more about the two that I just knew I wanted to introduce the world to how amazing they are, opossums in particular. I followed her for her work with neonatal kittens, but I stayed for the opossums, and I hope you appreciate the marvelous marsupials — like Gus — the way that I do.

I adore my wolves, too, and the concept of the hierarchy of the pack/feeding as a love language for shifters can be found in the entire universe. So, if you want to see other devoted, protective, possessive heroes like Max, I have plenty!

Never His Mate begins a rejected mates shifter series where the FMC and MMC find their way back to each other.

The Feral's Captive is the first in a trilogy where rejected mates find happiness with someone else (for books one and two... three is a little different).

Prey begins a four-book series that is my take on Little Red Riding Hood, only the big, bad wolf is the hero and granny is the villain.

And, of course, *Watch Me Burn* is similar in the vein of *Fake It 'Til You Mate It*. It features a fire witch heroine and a grumpy wolf shifter in a small shifter town in Alaska, where the residents hide out from supernatural threats, and the mayor is a skunk shifter who wears an air freshener around his neck!

Plus, there will be two more books in the **Murder in Moonburrow** series — keep reading/tapping/scrolling for a sneak peek at the blurb for book two, starring our favorite rascally raccoon Roxy!

xoxo,

Sarah

I NEVER KNEW ROOTING THROUGH THE TRASH WOULD LEAD TO THIS...

When Honey asks me to watch over Dough You Believe in Magic so she can go on an out-of-Moonburrow honeymoon with Sheriff Max, I reluctantly agree. We're kind of, sort of friends now, and I don't want to mess up her bakery, but the positive opossum insists that I can't... I knew better, but I said 'yes'.

I'm regretting that now.

It was a silly mistake. I tossed the keys into the

garbage, then threw it out in the dumpster. Good thing raccoons don't mind digging through the trash because, once I shift, I go searching — and find *another* dead body behind Honey's charmed bakery.

Only the gorgeous blond-haired, purple-eyed preppie opossum shifter isn't *dead* dead... though tell that to the ghost that steps out of the shadows right as I scramble out of the dumpster.

He's Ashton Morgan, Honey's cousin and an opossum who played dead and, somehow, his soul left his body. Now he wants to know who 'killed' him, how to break the curse that's keeping him from returning to his body, and how he ended up in Moonburrow in the first place—and he seems to think that I'm going to do everything I can to help him.

And, well, considering he's my fated mate, I think I'll have to before Ash goes from playing dead to *staying* dead.

PRE-ORDER NOW

SHE CAME TO MOONBURROW TO BREAK ONE CURSE — AND JUST MIGHT BE THE KEY TO BREAKING ANOTHER...

And because I just have to give Riordan a story, he will close out the trilogy!

KEEP IN TOUCH

Stay tuned for what's coming up next! Follow me at any of these places—or sign up for my newsletter—for news, promotions, upcoming releases, and more!

SarahSpadeBooks.com
Sarah's Newsletter
Sarah's Signed Book Store

facebook.com/sarahspadebooks
x.com/stressie
instagram.com/sarahspadebooks
amazon.com/author/sarahspade

ALSO BY SARAH SPADE

Holiday Hunk

Halloween Boo

This Christmas

Auld Lang Mine

I'm With Cupid

Getting Lucky

When Sparks Fly

Holiday Hunk: the Complete Series

Claws and Fangs

Leave Janelle

Never His Mate

Always Her Mate

Forever Mates

Hint of Her Blood

Taste of His Skin

Stay With Me

Never Say Never: Gem & Ryker

Bound by the Moon

Sanctuary

Watch Me Burn

Make Me Bleed

Beasts of Blackmoor

Trick or Beast

Christmas Eve with Krampus

Just Right

Big Bad Wolf

Murder in Moonburrow

Fake It 'Til You Mate It

Play Dead, Stay Dead

Of Murder and Magic

Claws Clause

(written as Jessica Lynch)

Mates 4*free*

Hungry Like a Wolf

Of Mistletoe and Mating

No Way

Season of the Witch

Rogue

Sunglasses at Night

Ain't No Angel

True Angel

Ghost of Jealousy

Night Angel

Broken Wings

Of Santa and Slaying

Lost Angel

Born to Run

Uptown Girl

A Pack of Lies

Here Kitty, Kitty

Ordinance 7304: the Bond Laws (Claws Clause Collection #1)

Living on a Prayer (Claws Clause Collection #2)

Diamonds are a Witch's Best Friend (Claws Clause Collection #3)